AFTER THE AUCTION

Linda Frank (signature)

AFTER THE
AUCTION

Linda Frank

Cover design by Dara England
Interior design by Cecile Kaufman

ISBN: 978-0-9844939-0-6

DEDICATION

To Friends and Family Whose
Love and Support Helped Make This Happen

You know who you are!

AFTER THE AUCTION

Contents

PART I

Chapter 1

Vienna, 1938

The little girl clung to her mother as three men in black leather coats stormed from room to room opening cabinets, pulling out drawers, kicking furniture with their boots, shouting. Suddenly, the young, black-haired one the others called "Obersturmführer Bucholz" announced, "We're done here."

As they swept past, the little girl struggled to break free, flailing her arms, pushing against her mother's grasp locked tightly around her middle. She screamed, ignoring her mother's whispered pleas to shush.

"The Seder plate. You can't take that. Papa, Papa, where are you going? No. No. Mama! Let me go. Look what they're doing."

New York City, March 1990

"No, No. That's our Seder plate. You can't do this."

There was no one to shush me, and I was barely aware that I'd leapt to my feet screaming until I heard the uproar around me. My sixty-year-old self had morphed back to the impulsive eight-year-old I was that night in 1938. To the last time I'd seen the antique Italian Seder plate that had just appeared on a pedestal on stage. The last time I saw my father—ever.

There was buzzing in the audience of about one hundred collectors, curators, and wannabes at an auction of Jewish ritual items. The gilded faux Versailles hotel ballroom looked like a tennis match as heads swung back and forth from me to the stage and back again.

The auctioneer, Shira Reznik, the head of the New York office of the Mosaica auction firm based in Israel, ignored me at first. A compact woman with frizzy red hair wearing a black pants suit, she maintained a tight smile and waited for the audience to quiet down. Finally, she had no choice. She held up her hands to calm the crowd as she visibly inhaled and addressed me.

"Excuse me, ma'am," said Reznik. "Is there a problem? Please take your seat so we can begin the bidding."

"A problem? Yes, there's a problem. That Seder plate belonged to my family. It was stolen by the Nazis. I saw them take it out of our apartment. You're selling stolen property!"

I sat down, suddenly winded, my heart pounding. I'm not sure which shocked me more—seeing the Seder plate or making such a spectacle of myself.

On stage Reznik turned her mouth away from the microphone and conferred with the man next to her, Professor Shaul Rotan. Rotan, a tall, stooped Judaica expert from Israel's Hebrew University, had made scholarly pronouncements all afternoon in his role as "permanent consultant to Mosaica." His accented English, to my poly-lingual ears, sounded like German roots mixed with Israeli Hebrew, a likely mix for a man that looked seventy-something.

When they finished their conversation, Rotan shot me a withering gaze, hoisted the Seder plate off its pedestal, and darted backstage behind the navy velvet curtain.

"Ladies and gentlemen," Reznik said as the curtain fluttered behind her, "this piece has been withdrawn, and the auction is now concluded." Gavel in hand, she immediately disappeared via the same route as the professor.

I shoved past the rows of seats toward the side entrance closest to the stage. Others in the audience glanced at me but avoided eye contact. There was only one exit out of the ballroom toward the elevator.

"What's with this rude lady?" I heard someone muttering.

Silently, two groups parted to open a Red Sea passage toward the foyer. It was empty except for a few people who'd left during my outburst. In vain I rushed toward the elevator bank and the door to a stairway exit. No Reznik or Rotan.

I stood alone for a moment, catching my breath. I was barely conscious of the snippets of conversation around me:

"Who is that woman? Damn, I wanted to bid on that Seder plate."

"Do you think she knows what she's talking about?"

"Did you see that Seder plate? My God. The picture in the catalogue was gorgeous, but up close. . . ."

The catalogue. I had picked one up on the way into the auction; it must have slipped off my lap when the Seder plate appeared. I slinked away from my rest stop and threaded my way against the flow of people treating me like an untouchable. I went back into the ballroom occupied only by hotel staff stacking chairs and lugging a vacuum cleaner.

The catalogue lay on the floor in front of my uncollected chair. I sat down again, no doubt to the annoyance of the crew, and flipped to the last page, the Seder plate's picture and description. Though it couldn't compare to the real thing, even a photograph showed how splendid this piece was.

Describing it as just a Seder plate failed to account for its grandeur. Certainly, it fulfilled its function as the bearer of Passover symbols to the Seder table. But its design and decoration made it unique—three tiers increasing in diameter from the top to the bottom, all crafted from the signature royal blue glass of the Venetian island of Murano. A sterling silver spine connected the tiers, which were edged in silver filigree encrusted with sapphires and pearls.

The smallest circle, on top, bore a groove to nestle a wine cup for the prophet, Elijah, mythically believed to visit every Seder. The second level held the three matzahs traditional to the ceremony. The six indentations in the large bottom tier displayed the foods that embody the Passover story—bitter herbs symbolizing the difficult life of slavery; salt water for slaves' tears; the lamb shank bone for the paschal lamb sacrificed; the pasty *charoses* mixture of fruit, nuts, and wine depicting the mortar the Jewish slaves used to build pyramids; a green vegetable representing spring harvest; and an egg signifying life.

Minus the silver Hebrew letters labeling each indentation, the Seder plate could have been an epergne for finger sandwiches and scones at high tea in a grand English country home. In fact, the catalogue write-up mentioned that its creator, Abramo di Salamone, crafted more pieces for secular use than for ritual.

Di Salamone was described as a master artisan of the sixteenth century. Although he lived in the walled quarter of Venice thought by some scholars to be the original "ghetto," his reputation filtered out of the Jewish community to the upper levels of Venetian society. Di Salamone creations found themselves in the palazzos of the ruling doges. This was interesting background information for the magazine assignment that had led me to the auction that day. But it wouldn't help me get the Seder plate back.

I closed the booklet and stuffed it into the black leather tote bag at my feet. I just sat there, feeling powerless either to figure out what to do next or even to get up and leave. I dropped my head, wrapped my arms around myself, and doubled over as if in pain. But it wasn't physical.

Suddenly, a slight smoker's cough announced the arrival of a pair of gray flannel legs rising from Italian tasseled loafers. I looked up to a face that was familiar, but I couldn't put a name to it. The face was craggy, not handsome, with a square protruding jaw line and dark complexion. Thinning black hair was slicked backward from the forehead to a length just above his collar, a style that aimed to make the most of what was left. Not more than five feet eight, build more solid than stocky, wearing the navy-blazer–blue-shirt-striped-rep-tie uniform, well-tailored and fine quality, but not dashing on this physique. He smiled down at me. And clapped his hands together in a slow rhythm.

"Bravo," said a deep voice that could probably boom, but was deliberately softened. "What a performance. I wanted to meet the mystery lady who stopped the show."

"This isn't Broadway," I said.

He stopped clapping and bent down, placing his right hand lightly on my shoulder.

"No, of course not. I'm sorry. I didn't mean to be flip. Really. What you said was serious."

"And I made quite a spectacle of myself in the process."

I looked around, saw the hotel staff glaring at us, and stood up.

"I suppose we should get out of here."

"Don't forget your pocketbook." He bent down to pick up my bag still on the floor next to the chair.

"Thanks. I'm so thrown—I don't know what I'm doing."

"It must have been quite a shock. And the Mosaica people took it seriously. Did you see the look of terror on Shira's Reznik's face? Even that snooty old professor looked scared. You got to them. Stopping the auction right away—that's unheard of."

"And not staying around to talk to me? That only makes me more suspicious."

"Have you ever done business with them?"

"No. I only came because I'm writing an article on the Judaica market."

"You're a writer? Have I heard of you?"

"I don't know. Professionally, I use the name Lily Weinberg, my maiden name. Otherwise, I'm Lily Kovner. And you?"

"Simon Rieger."

Of course. The scion of Rieger & Co., a decades-old purveyor of jewelry rivaling Tiffany or Harry Winston. A business known among the cognoscenti for its chic lounge in the back of a Madison Avenue shop—a relaxed setting where regular clients could shop privately at custom prices. I'd read about a messy divorce—and endowed university chairs and other top-dollar philanthropy. His photograph appeared regularly in the Evenings feature of the *Times* Sunday Styles section, usually arm in arm with some stunning woman. Actually, different stunning women, all younger than he. What was he doing talking to me?

"Kovner. Kovner. Arthur Kovner?"

"Arthur was my husband."

"A fine man. Brilliant. His economic consulting firm did a research project on my industry a few years ago. I heard about his death. How long ago?"

"Just a year."

"I'm sorry for your loss. And, from what you said today, you must be a Holocaust victim," he said, glancing at my left wrist.

There's no number burned into my skin. It's funny, but I don't think of myself as a victim, or even as a Survivor. I was deported to Britain on the *Kindertransport*, a luxurious adventure on commercial railroad and ferry with other children and kind chaperones to a safe destination—in my case the loving open arms of an aunt and uncle. It couldn't compare to the horrors of the boxcars. But the Seder plate's fleeting reappearance had resurrected memories of life "before," and the loss of it all.

"No, not a victim—I never use that term. Although I am the only survivor of my immediate family. I wasn't in the camps, if that's what you mean. My parents and grandparents were murdered, but I got out several months after Vienna fell."

"You must have been quite young at the time. How can you remember the Nazis taking that Seder plate?"

"If you'd lived through a night like that, you'd understand. I was eight years old. We all loved that Seder plate. When the Nazis stormed in . . . carried it off . . . you just don't forget. They took my father, too. It was. . . . " I felt myself tearing up. "Believe me, you'd remember."

Simon Rieger drew back and took a breath. "I didn't mean to upset you. I apologize; that was stupid."

"You don't have to apologize. How would you know? Count yourself lucky not to know."

He nodded.

"Listen, it's been nice meeting you, but I've got to get out of here and try to catch up with the Mosaica people. Get to their office."

"It's four-thirty on Sunday afternoon. They won't be there. But we can call to check."

We were standing near a pay phone. He fished in his trousers pocket, pulled out a quarter, and handed it to me. The number was on the back of the catalogue.

He stood by while I dialed and listened to a recording that spelled out Mosaica's normal business hours and announced the auction that had just concluded.

"You're right. They're closed until tomorrow morning."

"Why don't we go downstairs and have a drink?"

I shook my head. "I really appreciate the invitation, but I need to get home and figure out what I'm going to do about this. I wouldn't be good company."

Handing me his card, he said, "I might be able to help you. Perhaps we can get together another time."

Sure, I thought, Simon Rieger is going to ask me out for a drink again. Most single women my age, knowing his preference for dates who appeared young enough to be our daughters—and his—would sacrifice their firstborn for this invitation. I told myself that it was a polite one-time gesture inspired by pity over my dilemma.

"That would be nice," I murmured as I fished for my own card, which he actually read.

"You've written for *New York* and the *New Yorker*, haven't you? And the *Times?*"

"All of the above, occasionally. I was a staff reporter at the old *Herald Tribune* and later at the *Village Voice*. Just freelancing now. Gives me the luxury of working when I want to on assignments that interest me or something I want to pitch to an editor."

"Which is this?"

"An assignment. The *Smithsonian Magazine*. On Judaica collectors and sales, rising prices, old European pieces showing up on the market. If you're here, it must mean you're a collector. Should I interview you?"

"I *am* a collector, and, yes, you should interview me. If you had a drink with me, you could start now."

I was tempted, but the heft of the Mosaica catalogue in my bag reminded me of the weight on my mind.

"Please give me a rain check. This just isn't a good time."

We shook hands goodbye. From the Waldorf lobby he headed toward the Lexington Avenue exit. I walked out onto Park Avenue and turned north, hoping that the brisk air of the March dusk would clarify the conflict raging in my head.

On the one hand, this was the story of a lifetime. On the other, emotional entanglement and upheaval could compromise my professionalism. I was no Hunter Thompson or Nellie Bly—I'd never inject myself into a story.

My professionalism? What was the matter with me? This was my life and my family's property stolen by the Nazis. Story or no story, I had to act.

But did I need this in my life? Although widowhood was no picnic, watching Arthur suffer had made the inevitable end a blessing for him. Pancreatic cancer doesn't give anyone a lot of time to reflect. You try to fight it as best you can, but the outcome is unequivocal from the beginning. Deprived of the "golden years" we'd anticipated, I carried on, resuming a routine revolving around family, friends, volunteer work, culture, and travel that we'd hoped to enjoy together and had planned to share for a long time.

After my hiatus as caregiver, I'd started to work again and had just published a piece in *USA Today* (of all places!) about managing a terminally ill loved one at home. The *Smithsonian* assignment was a clean break from the official year of mourning and saying Kaddish. I missed Arthur terribly and still sometimes anguished over how unfair and painful his illness was. But that level of grief had dwindled to waves lasting just hours or even moments. Self-reliance had resumed its place as my best friend.

Yet, I had doubts about whether to pursue the Seder plate. Was my sense of balance steady enough? Would this catapult me back into the bleakness I experienced right after Arthur died?

Did I have a choice?

The Seder plate symbolized my heritage, not as a valuable *objet d'art* but as a tangible remembrance of my childhood and of the parents who were squashed like mosquitoes by the Nazis. Cavalier as I was about the victim label, I couldn't help but be staggered by the hatbox of memory, long shoved onto a high shelf, that suddenly toppled down on my head.

I had to get the Seder plate back.

The air felt good, and it would be a pleasant walk to my apartment on Central Park South. But I needed to go somewhere else—fast.

"Taxi," I yelled, plucking the catalogue from my bag to give the driver Mosaica's address.

Chapter 2

TRUE TO THE message on its answering machine, the office of Mosaica, a storefront gallery with a security admittance button, was shut tight. The space was dark, and even if Professor Rotan and Ms. Reznik were in a back room, my buzzing went unanswered.

I knew this would be a wild goose chase. They wouldn't be so foolish as to go straight back there. But I had to give it a shot to convince myself that I was pursuing every avenue as quickly as possible.

Heading back downtown, I drifted west to Park Avenue, a busier and more visible street to walk alone as dusk eased into evening. This was Mayor Dinkins's Manhattan. In the past few years, homeless people, many chronically mentally ill, had appeared on the street, intimidating pedestrians into giving them handouts. Crime reached an all-time high. Tourists emerging from after-theatre suppers were robbed at gunpoint. The vicious "Central Park jogger" rape of the previous year still gnawed at everyone's consciousness. Accustomed as I was to the vagaries of the city I loved, I knew to watch my back and cradle my bag like a football.

I was only going to Sixty-eighth Street, between Park and Madison. I bounded up the few stairs to the varnished black door of a classic brownstone as venerable as its owner.

"Lily, such a delightful surprise!"

The old man in the leather chair reading the Sunday *Times* had left Warsaw for good in 1939 and spoke English well, but his syntax still betrayed his roots.

He beckoned me over for a kiss after his weekend housekeeper ushered me into the library.

"How are you, Uncle?"

"Good, good, for an old guy. Better now you're here. I'm having Estelle order Chinese pretty soon. Sunday night. You'll stay, of course?"

"Sure, you know me, the freeloader. Why do you think I dropped in at this hour?"

Nachman Tanski laughed heartily. At ninety-six he looked remarkably similar to when I first met him over fifty years earlier—better in some ways. He still sported a neatly trimmed mustache, but his face was barely lined, and his former paunch had diminished. Always impeccably turned out, he wore black slacks and a gray cashmere sweater. In his prime he was only about five feet six; age had shrunk him down at least four inches. I'm five five, and I could kiss the top of a head that even photos from sixty years ago revealed to be bald.

I'd started calling him "Uncle" when I first arrived in London. He was living there in the early days of the war, a refugee like me. Aunt Lottie and Uncle Arnold invited him often, and he occasionally treated me to a children's performance at the theatre or ballet before moving on to New York City a few years later. Once I came to the States, married to Arthur, he permanently assumed the role of uncle, or surrogate father. A lifelong bachelor, he cherished the memory of the one great love of his life—my mother.

Outside his house was New York City in the 1890s. Inside it could have been Paris 1930, authentically Art Deco, replicating the décor of his mansion in Warsaw, and still packed with priceless paintings and *objets d'art*, including Judaica, despite having donated or sold significant chunks of his collection. Uncle had abandoned his Warsaw house and its contents in August of 1939, two weeks before the Germans attacked Poland. He had traveled to the final prewar Zionist Congress in Geneva, the last congress for many years.

At the meeting the delegates, fully cognizant of what was about to befall European Jews and anguished by Britain's strict limits on Jewish immigration to Palestine, agonized over their inability to rescue them. When the meeting adjourned, Uncle simply left Switzerland for his flat in London, never to return to the art-packed Polish house that delighted Nazi looters a month later.

"Something's wrong, I can see it from your face," he said to me now. "That same determined look. Like when you were a little girl."

"I'm in shock. You won't believe what happened." I sat down on the ottoman alongside his outstretched legs.

"Nu, so tell me," he said, folding the business section on his lap.

"I went to a Judaica auction at the Waldorf this afternoon for work. I think I told you—I've got an assignment from the *Smithsonian Magazine*. The auction was great for the story. Until they brought out the last piece . . . it was that Seder plate you brought us when I was a little girl. You remember it, don't you?"

"Who could forget it? It was a di Salamone; I bought a menorah of his at the same time. Of course, the menorah . . . " his hand flung out dismissively ". . . lost in Warsaw. That Seder plate—that was a special gift for your mother. What year?"

"1937. The last Seder before. . . . " Tears welled up in my eyes. I looked at Uncle; he remembered, too.

"Yes, 1937," he said quietly.

I composed myself. "Uncle, do you realize that I hadn't seen the Seder plate since the Nazi soldiers came to our apartment and took it away at the same time they took my father? It's stolen property. This auction house is trying to sell property that belongs to my family. It belongs to me."

"You're right, darling. A serious matter. Did you tell the people running the auction? Whose auction was it?"

"Mosaica. They're based in Tel Aviv, but with a New York branch."

"I know the name. Of course, for me, always Sotheby's."

"The manager of the office here and a professor from Hebrew University were running the auction. I made quite a spectacle of myself leaping to my feet and accusing them of selling something stolen. Then they shut it down. The professor snatched the Seder plate off the stage, and they both disappeared."

"What do you mean 'disappeared'?"

"I ran to the elevator, but they were gone already. And just now, before I came here, I went up to the Mosaica office on First Avenue. It was closed up tight. But I do have the catalogue." I pulled it out of my bag and flipped to the last page.

"Yes," said Uncle, quiet again after glancing at the photo and handing the booklet back to me. "Who could forget it?"

I opened the front and came across a listing of Mosaica's management.

"This is interesting, the names of the people who run the auction house. Short write-ups on them. The top person—someone named Eliezer Ben-Shuvah. He received a degree from Cambridge. Here's one on Rotan. . . . "

"Who?"

"Professor Shaul Rotan, emeritus from Hebrew University's Judaica department. He was the professor I mentioned who was on stage at the auction. He has a degree from Cambridge. Maybe that's how they met."

"Rotan I've heard of," said Uncle. "He does what for this Mosaica?"

"Permanent Consulting Scholar is his title."

"Whatever that means. Probably a good deal financially. Hebrew U. doesn't pay very well. And who was the other person running the auction?"

"Shira Reznik, manager of the New York office. Not a Cambridge grad, Columbia, with a master's in Jewish art from the Jewish Theological Seminary."

Just then, the doorbell signaled the arrival of the Shun Lee deliveryman. Uncle got up and led me into the dining room. Even for Chinese take-out the table setting maintained the elegant standard of this household—candlelight, red brocade place mats, ivory and silver chopsticks, bone china plates and tea cups, crystal water goblets. Estelle carried in the familiar white containers on silver platters.

Once seated, Uncle plopped three steamed dumplings—my favorite—on my plate.

"I need to find these people to find the Seder plate. It showed up one second and just vanished again. I wonder if I dreamed it all."

"Don't be silly. You have the catalogue—you know it's real. But you'll need your strength. Eat!"

Nibbling a pot sticker, I spit out a name. "Bucholz."

"Bucholz? What's that?"

"The name of the Nazi officer who looted our apartment and took my father and the Seder plate."

"You remember that? You were what—seven?"

"Eight. The name is written in Mama's album."

"Ah," he said, "of course. Elisabeth's album."

Uncle knew about my mother's record of important family and historical events from the time I was born until I left Vienna. It consisted of newspaper clippings, photographs, and her written commentary, and was packed in my suitcase for the *Kindertransport*. I'd ignore it for years, until a nostalgic or lonely mood would lead me to pull it out. That had happened often since Arthur's death.

"I picked it up last week and reread the part about the night the Nazis came. I really need to have that scrapbook fixed. The leather on the cover is all scratched, and a lot of the pages are ripped."

"Such a long time," Uncle said. "And you still look at it."

"Honestly, the older I get, the more I pull it out. Maybe I'm reaching for her."

"Maybe that's what finding the Seder plate is all about." Uncle arched his eyebrows.

As a child, I thought my mother didn't care about me as much as my father did. She could be withdrawn and snappish. When she deposited me on the *Kindertransport* and didn't come to retrieve me in London after months had passed, I thought she had deliberately abandoned me. Her writing straightened me out by revealing the depth of her character and intellect and the pride and pleasure she felt as my parent. Her decision to send me off must have been wrenching. She had already lost my father, and her twin brother had left for Shanghai. Staying in Austria was a death sentence she'd tried to evade but hadn't, out of duty to her elderly parents. To part with her child, the single source of joy in an atmosphere that was already grim and would soon become desolate, was a selfless sacrifice to guarantee my survival.

Uncle served me a generous portion of eggplant in garlic sauce and then helped himself.

"Such a precious gift your mother gave you . . . life. Twice—once when she gave birth and again when she sent you on the *Kindertransport*. That album, it's a gift, too. She was. . . . " He dabbed his eyes with a damask napkin.

"I know." I stabbed a chunk of eggplant with my chopsticks and stared at the candlelight, lost in memory for a moment and giving him time to compose himself.

"Uncle, the Seder plate. With the name of the Nazi who led the looting party, can't I find out what happened to him through someone like Simon Wiesenthal? You know him, don't you?"

"Wiesenthal? Certainly. I've got his private number. But I'll call first to tell him to take your call. Still such a busy man, driven. This Nazi hunting never ends. Dangerous business. Not child's play like . . . like . . . like hunting for the Afikomen."

"Afikomen! That's great, Uncle. The perfect code name for my search."

The *Afikomen,* literally meaning *dessert,* is a piece of matzah hidden early in the Seder, then hunted for by the children at the end. Hiding the Afikomen might symbolize the scattered twelve tribes of Israel. At least, that's one of the theories. In most families it gives children a reason to stay alert during the ceremony. The winner of the hunt gets a prize—a little money or some other treat.

Uncle laughed. "Oy, a code name. What am I going to do with you, Lily?"

"Oh, I almost forgot, I met another Simon today—Simon Rieger."

"The jewelry man? At the auction? I know he collects. We were on the Jewish Museum board together. So, what did he have to say for himself?"

"He was very solicitous about the Seder plate and offered to help me. I don't know if he was serious. He did invite me out for a drink, but I wanted to take off quickly. I don't think I'm his type."

When I got home from Uncle's after dinner, I decided to call my children. Reaching my son, Jacob, in San Francisco was always a hit-or-miss proposition between the difference in time zones and his schedule. The moment he picked up the phone, I knew that I'd guessed wrong again. It was bath time. I heard my daughter-in-law, Amy, in the background pleading with Gabriella and Joshua, their three-year-old twins, to stop splashing each other. This signaled that it would not be a long conversation.

"Hi, Mom. A hectic time around here." California had not altered my son's staccato speech style.

"I can tell. They sound pretty hyper."

"Long day. Purim carnival at temple, they dressed up, the works."

"Purim? Already? I guess so, it's March. Did they go as Queen Esther and the king?"

"Josh had to be Haman."

"What a little devil! If I were really a good grandmother, I would have baked hamentashen to send them."

"You're a wonderful grandmother, Mom, don't worry. They had plenty today, got really sticky in the process. Anything new?"

"Well, only that this afternoon I went to an auction and saw the Seder plate that the Nazis stole from us fifty-two years ago. It came on the block, then was withdrawn after I made a fuss."

"That Seder plate that you talk about—the one Uncle gave to your parents? Wow! Shocking! Did you get it back?"

"Not yet. The people running the auction took off with it. I've got to find them."

"Unreal. Sorry, Mom, I'd like to talk but I've got to help Amy with the kids. And I'm on call. Terminal little boy in the hospital."

"I understand, I just wanted to let you know," I said, resigned to the inevitable brief conversation.

"Call my sister, the investigative reporter. And you're no slouch. The two of you will put your heads together, figure it out. Let me know if I can help."

"Thanks, dear. You're all still coming for Passover, aren't you?"

"Got the tickets. The twins are learning the Four Questions. Can't wait to show off for Grandma."

It was too late to call my daughter, Elizabeth, in London. I'd consumed the Sunday *Times* hours ago before the auction. I picked up a magazine but couldn't concentrate. Sleep was out of the question. Talking about Purim had reminded me that I hadn't sent my kids any "care packages" lately. I needed to do something I could manage without much thinking, an activity to keep me busy and accomplish something until I got sleepy.

Precisely when I'd started plopping spoonfuls of cookie dough onto a baking sheet, goopy batter on my hands, the phone rang.

"Hello, Lily, this is Simon Rieger."

"Oh, hello," trying sound nonchalant, despite my surprise and the buttery mess I was depositing on the receiver.

"I want to help out your research, so how about starting our interview by having dinner with me tomorrow night?"

"That would be nice."

He named a restaurant on the East Side, and we agreed to meet there, after I remembered a five o'clock appointment with my accountant.

"Are you sure you don't want me to pick you up?"

Somehow, I didn't link chivalry with a ladies' man.

"Positive. See you there, Simon."

By the time I climbed into bed after midnight, I'd baked dozens of cookies, packed them to send to my two sets of far-flung children, and in the process eaten at least four myself. I'd better watch it, I thought. I need to find the Seder plate before I gain twenty pounds, which will guarantee that Simon Rieger would want nothing to do with me.

Drifting off to sleep, I dreamed—what was it? Something about my mother as a young woman . . . the Seder plate . . . Uncle.

PART II

Vienna 1925–1941

Chapter 3

THE PICTURE GALLERY, Elisabeth thought, what a deceptive name for room after room of masterpieces by the most famous European artists of the previous six centuries. No matter how often she visited the Kunsthistorisches Museum, the maze of treasures inspired both admiration and revulsion.

Admiration at the scope of the collections accumulated by the ruling Hapsburgs. Revulsion at the acquisitive decadence in an empire so chronically short of money that even this monument to Emperor Franz Josef's dream took twenty years to construct, starting and stopping with the erratic flow of funds. The result was an elaborate palace—two rectangular wings of marble, stone, and gold leaf, topped by a dome worthy of the Vatican. Across the verdant Maria Theresa Platz stood the Natural History Museum, a structure not only built simultaneously but with an identical exterior.

Although the emperor and the empire itself had both expired since the end of the Great War, Elisabeth could imagine the old man holding court on one of the two parallel marble balconies that connected the wings of the Picture Gallery. To take in all of the rooms of both wings one needed to cross back and forth at least twice.

Elisabeth had noticed, going the opposite way on the opposite balcony, a chubby balding man with a small dark mustache. Both times he smiled at her, and, despite his less than ideal looks, Elisabeth smiled back.

It was a game, like comic operetta, the damsel and the unlikely beau pursuing her, but always going the opposite way. Why not have a little fun? With the number of rooms on each side, she figured that she and the man would never meet. Until she stood staring at a Rembrandt self-portrait and found the man next to her. Right next to her, as he was barely an inch taller.

Up close he looked younger, his face and nearly hairless head soft-skinned, and his physique more solid than fat. His beige linen summer suit bore the creases of the sweltering summer weather, despite the quality of its fabric.

"Hello," he said with a Polish accent, like that of her mother's seamstress in the Leopoldstadt district.

"Hello."

"Do you visit the museum often?"

"Yes. I am concentrating on art history at the university. I love it here."

"That's why you're taking notes," he said, his eyes following her hands replacing a tiny notebook into her purse.

"Yes. And what about you? Do you come here often?"

"Whenever I come to Vienna. I live in Warsaw."

"Oh."

Elisabeth, normally neither shy nor coy, couldn't believe that she felt too flustered to deliver a more dazzling reply. There was something about this man that attracted her in a strange way. Not that her experience with the opposite sex was vast. Although her mother was forever dredging up young men whose social standing met her requisites, the daughter preferred casual outings to local cafés with fellow students, discussing art and politics.

He said, "Do you like Rembrandt?"

"Of the Old Masters he's my favorite. But the more I learn, I find that my taste runs to modern art."

"Really?" The man seemed genuinely interested. "Like which artists, tell me."

"The Impressionists . . . Matisse," she said, finding her persona in the conversation. "I have seen some of the paintings by that Spaniard, Picasso, but I don't like them so well as Matisse or Monet."

"Do you know the work of Gustav Klimt from here in Vienna?"

"Oh, yes," she said. "Everyone has heard of Klimt. I love his use of colorful patterns. Of course, the moderns will never show up in this museum. But there are treasures here. The Hapsburgs weren't good rulers, but they knew how to collect art."

"You are very knowledgeable, Miss . . . ?"

"Heilbrun."

"Miss Heilbrun, my name is Nachman Tanski."

"Please call me Elisabeth."

"A lovely name, Elisabeth. Like the great queen of England."

"In my case, our empress, the tragic one with the famous nickname Sisi. So, my name is spelled with an 's,' not a 'z.' My parents are such patriotic Austrians always talking about the old empire and royal family. You would think they were aristocrats, instead of Jews."

Nachman laughed but changed the subject.

"Would you do me the honor of taking coffee with me? I believe the café in the museum is quite pleasant. Shall we go over there?"

Without actually touching her, he guided Elisabeth out of the gallery.

Seated over coffee and pastry, she asked, "What are you doing here in Vienna? It's hardly the most pleasant place to holiday in August."

"I am a delegate to the Fourteenth Zionist Congress. We are meeting at the Wiener Concert Hall."

"What is that? I have never heard that word, 'Zionist.'"

Nachman laughed so hard he almost spit out the coffee *mit schlag* he had just sipped.

"In Vienna you have never heard of Zionism? You live in the city of Theodor Herzl, the father of Zionism."

Elisabeth was taken aback and offended by his mockery.

"Well, forgive my ignorance, but I don't know who Theodor Herzl is, either."

Her companion, realizing that his reaction had been hurtful, apologized.

"Oh, I'm sorry. He died in 1904. . . . ."

"The year I was born. Maybe that's why his name isn't familiar to me."

"Yes, yes, no doubt. But in Zionism Theodor Herzl left a great legacy for the Jewish people. Herzl was a journalist and a playwright who came here from Budapest as a teenager and studied at your university. He saw such anti-Semitism as a student there and when he covered the Dreyfus trial in Paris. It convinced him that we need our own homeland. Europe, Russia—these are not places for us to stay."

"I've heard of Dreyfus. That poor French captain who was wrongfully accused and had to spend years on Devil's Island before the truth came out. Where did Herzl think this homeland should be?"

"First, maybe Uganda in Africa, as a temporary place for Russian Jews to escape pogroms. But the ultimate goal—Palestine. That's the place for the Jewish state."

Nachman's passion impressed Elisabeth.

"And you're a follower of this Zionist movement? So involved that you have come all the way to Vienna in the summer for a meeting of Zionists? Is this your work?"

"Oh, no. Hardly. Zionism is bad for my work. It takes a lot of time and money. I travel to these meetings, then I feel compelled to donate funds to help people who want to go to Palestine or who are already there. They have to work very hard. The land is arid, the swamps need draining. Just living in harmony with the Arabs is a trial. But, fortunately, I have the means for this, and it's very important to me. It should be a goal for all Jews."

The waiter came over to offer them more coffee and pastry. Elisabeth shook her head no, but Nachman took another steaming cupful topped with a generous puff of thick *schlag*. He did pass on a second helping of torte after a longing look at the pastry cart as it rolled away from the table.

"Such conviction," Elisabeth said. "I admire people who are devoted to a cause. Some of my friends are Socialists, some Communists, but I don't know of any who are Zionists."

"Maybe you'd be interested in coming to the Congress tomorrow? I can get you a pass to sit in the visitors' gallery."

"Really? Yes, I would. It sounds fascinating."

To think, she thought, that I almost didn't come to the museum today, because my mother wanted me to go shopping for a ball gown that I don't need for two months. If I even go to the silly ball at all.

"Well, you will see if it's fascinating. A lot of arguing and shouting goes on, I warn you."

"Oh, I'm used to arguing. I do it all the time with my mother, and my friends argue about politics and even art."

"Art? What's there to argue about in art, compared to politics?"

"The politics of art, among other things. That surprises you? Klimt, for instance. You mentioned him. Believe me, not everyone loves Klimt."

"I bought a small Klimt this morning," Nachman said quietly.

"You collect art then?"

"Yes, a bit. I am building a new home in Warsaw and I want some of the newer masters—like Klimt."

Elisabeth looked at her wristwatch.

"Oh, dear, look what time it is already. I must be going," she said rising from the table, "I enjoyed our discussion. Thank you."

And she disappeared down the marble staircase, leaving Nachman staring after her.

Elisabeth's spirits, buoyed by her afternoon with a man who not only offered interesting conversation but also listened to her and seemed genuinely interested in what she had to say, stayed high all the way home on the streetcar. By the time she arrived, it was nearly seven o'clock.

Pushing open the heavy wooden door of the Heilbrun family's large apartment, she heard her parents talking and a strange male voice responding.

"Oh, Elisabeth, here you are," her father said.

Her mother looked her over, pulled her close, and hissed, "I was worried. And look at your dress all crushed and sticky. You need to wash and change for dinner." Then, audible to the others, "Darling, Elisabeth, we have a guest for dinner, your father's young colleague, Dr. Weinberg. You've had a long day, dear, we will all excuse you if you want to freshen up."

Elisabeth nodded to the handsome young doctor. Was it her imagination, or did he really bow and click his heels like some impoverished count when he rose from the blue brocade-covered settee? Barely able to contain her amusement, she exited quickly to prevent herself from bursting out laughing. How long could she stall in the bathtub before reappearing? Not long enough.

The evening passed in typical Heilbrun style. A heavy dinner, despite several cold dishes designed to lighten it up in deference to August. The guest, Jacob Weinberg, preferred to be called "Jack," like an American. Despite his self-described origins as the son of "traditional" Jews in Galicia, a region that the war had shifted from the now-defunct Austro-Hungarian Empire to Polish rule, this Jack had adapted the pretensions of an assimilated Viennese Jew, like his hosts. Elisabeth wondered if he really believed what he was spewing, or if he was just trying to worm his way into her father's good graces to advance his career.

Her mother, as always, led the charge. "And where are you living here in Vienna, Dr. Weinberg?"

"Only about ten blocks from here, Mrs. Heilbrun. Close to the hospital, so I can get in very quickly, if there is an emergency in the middle of the night."

"Lodgings right here in Alsergrund. Excellent. You wouldn't want to be in the wrong neighborhood."

"Like Leopoldstadt, Mama?" Elisabeth sometimes egged her mother on.

"Elisabeth, what's wrong with you? No one we know would live there. Except, of course, Masha, the dressmaker, and Mr. Katz, your father's tailor." Turning to the guest, she continued, "That's the really Jewish district. *Our* friends live around here, as we both have all of our lives. Isn't that so, Oscar?"

"Absolutely, Gertrude," said Elisabeth's father. "You know, Jack, being at the university hospital, we Jewish doctors are careful about such things. Of course, we are the best doctors they've got, but we wouldn't want to be seen as '*yids*,' if you know what I mean."

Jack nodded in assent and launched into a monologue about the cultural advantages in Vienna.

"In Lemberg, where I come from," he said, "you wouldn't find Jews as patrons of the arts. They wouldn't be caught dead visiting a museum. Not that there was much to visit there. My father pooh-poohed all that. He just worked in his watchmaker shop all week and went to shul on Shabbos. My mother cooked and kept house, read only prayers, never a novel or history book. I couldn't wait to get out of there. I was born to live in a city like Vienna."

Elisabeth rolled her eyes toward the wall so that nobody could see her. What a phony! His poor parents had probably slaved and sacrificed for their accomplished, but ungrateful, progeny.

All of a sudden, Jack turned to her and asked, "Would you do me the honor of accompanying me to the opera next Saturday evening? I am told that the new production of *Don Giovanni* is quite good."

Aha! It finally dawned on Elisabeth that he had been invited as a potential suitor for her. She hated it when her parents did that. Did they think she would never find a husband on her own? She knew that she was pretty and attractive to men. Only twenty-one, hardly a spinster, she would graduate from the university in June. She wanted to use her degree, perhaps work at an art gallery, maybe even open one herself.

Before she could answer, her mother accepted for her.

"Of course, she will go with you. We were at the opera last week, and everyone looked so summery with the new bobbed hair. . . ."

Her father squelched this monologue. "Oh, you two will so enjoy the production. And that new tenor—Gertrude, do you remember his name?— the best I have ever heard, except for Caruso, of course."

"You heard Caruso sing?" Jack perked up. "Where, here in Vienna?"

"Twice. Once in Vienna and once in Milano, at La Scala, on our honeymoon, He was a marvel, but this new fellow. . . ."

"Tauber," Gertrude exclaimed. "Richard Tauber."

"A Jew, I've heard." Elisabeth could not resist. It was the only act of rebellion she could inject into the evening. To refute her mother's acceptance of Jack's invitation would only invite trouble. It was easier to keep the peace. The young doctor was handsome, and she enjoyed opera. She'd give him the benefit of the doubt—maybe he would be better company away from her mother.

Chapter 4

THE NEXT DAY, as they entered the Zionist Conference, Elisabeth pointed out to Nachman the German inscription above the door of Weiner Concert Hall.

"'Honour your German masters, then you preserve good spirits,'" she translated. This was a line from Richard Wagner's *Die Meistersänger*.

"After all that the Germans dragged us through in the war, this should have been scraped off," she said.

"The Germans will be trouble again," her companion replied. "Especially to the Jews."

The Wiener Concert Hall was one of Vienna's newer public spaces, opened in 1913, and its vast halls reflected the burgeoning audience for culture that came with the growth of the city's middle class around the turn of the century. Its programming also suited modern times. Richard Strauss had composed a special work for the opening concert, and new names such as Arnold Schoenberg and Erich Korngold débuted compositions there. But, when Elisabeth and Nachman entered the great hall that morning, the clatter was more public market than music hall. Though the session hadn't gaveled to a start, noisy debate had opened.

Nachman deposited her in the visitors' area on the first balcony before taking his seat in the delegates' section below. The rectangular hall, which seated 800, was packed. Amazed at the size of the crowd, Elisabeth observed that Nachman seemed to be one of the youngest and the best dressed, wearing an obviously custom tailored version of the new short jacket suits in vogue since the war. Among his colleagues were relics from the age of the Emperor, including a coterie sporting small goatees and old-fashioned waistcoats and holding top hats. They conferred next to a trio, boisterously gesturing as they spoke, in khaki work shirts and pants. Only a handful wore the black coats and hats and long beards typical of religious Jews. Elisabeth counted three women on the delegates' floor but many more seated in her section and in the balconies that protruded from the sides of the hall. The older women mostly looked like her mother and her friends, wearing ankle-length skirts, fitted jackets, and unwieldy straw hats trimmed in silk flowers. There were a few fashionable younger ones who, like Elisabeth, displayed light chemise frocks and cloche hats, but inconspicuous skirts and blouses dominated.

Looking around, she was surprised to see a few friends from the university and two of her father's medical colleagues. But most astonishing was the arrival of her twin brother, Erich, with his roommate at law school, Heinz Guttmann, from Berlin. As their eyes met, Erich made a beeline for his sister and greeted her with a hug and an obvious question.

"What are you doing here?"

"I could ask you the same thing," she said.

"I plead guilty to enticing your brother here," said the handsome Heinz, a longtime object of Elisabeth's secret and unrequited crush. "Who brought you, Elisabeth?"

"I came with a delegate, Nachman Tanski, from Warsaw. He is down there—see—waving to me."

"Tanski, huh?" Heinz was impressed. "He's an up-and-comer in the leadership ranks. Very wealthy, too."

"Elisabeth, how did you meet this man?" Erich was posturing as big brother, despite the two-minute age difference between them.

"At the Art History Museum. Yesterday. We went to the café for a while."

"Oh, so you just meet someone and right away have coffee with him and then go with him to a meeting the next day?"

"What's wrong with that? These are public places. You would do the same," she said.

"But I am not a woman."

"What does that have to do with it? It's 1925, Erich. Even Mother and Father allow me to leave the house on my own."

"Speaking of our dear parents, do they know where you are?"

"Do they know where *you* are?"

"No, of course not."

"Same here. And neither of us will tell them, will we?"

"Of course not. See you later, Elisabeth."

The gavel summoned the delegates to their seats. This was the Fourteenth Congress of the World Zionist Organization. Presiding was a well-dressed bald middle-aged man with pointy goatee, Dr. Chaim Weizmann, the organization's president. He opened the session by calling on a member from Brussels to introduce the first item on the agenda—whether to channel the organization's limited financial resources toward resettling Russian Jews in Palestine in the cities or in cooperative agricultural experiments called kibbutzim, where members struggled to pull miracles out of land that was either swampy or arid.

"We cannot rely on the cities to provide jobs and sustenance. The country needs to be developed. What these *chalutzim*—these pioneers—are doing will show the world that Jews can be farmers and achieve the Socialist dream," said a Czech speaker.

"Yes, because it is working so well in the new Soviet Union," came the retort of a Russian colleague. "Where the socialist geniuses who have replaced the czar already surpass him in deceit, cruelty, and anti-Semitism."

"Which is why your countrymen who are now flocking to Palestine should prove that it can work, free of those aberrations. We owe it to our brethren on the kibbutzim to invest in their efforts."

"But the cities will provide the political and cultural fabric of the society," replied the Russian. "We Jews have always prided ourselves on that. You're a fine one to speak. When do you plan to abandon your precious Prague for the swamps of the Galilee?"

Two hours of such acrimonious debate passed before Elisabeth knew it. She put away her ever-present notebook, into which she had scribbled the main points of the arguments and some questions. The session would break for lunch and reconvene in the afternoon. Nachman turned around, waved when he caught her eye, and pointed toward the main entrance as their meeting point, while inching his way up the aisle chatting with fellow delegates.

"Well, Miss Heilbrun, what did you think about the debate?"

"This is a new world for me. I have never realized that Jews were so engaged in issues of the Jewish people in a larger sense. It is fascinating. Have you been to Palestine?"

"Yes, three times since 1919. The last time this past April for the opening of a new university in Jerusalem, the Hebrew University."

"The Hebrew University! Imagine," said Elisabeth.

"You have heard, I assume, of Albert Einstein and Dr. Freud."

"Yes, of course."

"They are both on the board of governors of the Hebrew University, along with Dr. Weizmann, who presided this morning."

"Who is he?"

"A brilliant chemist, but now he devotes most of his time to the Zionist movement. Our spokesman, the ambassador of the Jewish people, highly respected. Weizmann has entrée in the upper echelons of international politics. He's even met with Faisal, the Arab king."

Elisabeth pointed to the portrait of a dark-haired bearded man hanging above the stage. "Who is that?"

"Theodor Herzl, our founder, whom I mentioned yesterday. Come, let's have lunch. I've made reservations at the Sacher Hotel. Perhaps we can sit on their terrace."

"Don't your colleagues expect you to lunch with them?"

"Not when the alternative is lunch with an intelligent and beautiful young woman."

As they walked and soon sat down at a prime terrace table at the legendary hotel's main restaurant, the conversation continued to revolve around Zionism. Elisabeth was an eager pupil, peppering her tutor with questions.

"If Dr. Weizmann has entrée to the upper echelons of some governments, has he made any progress?"

"Well, one would say that the Balfour Declaration was progress."

"And that is?"

"In 1917 the British government made a proclamation announcing that it viewed with favor the establishment of a Jewish state in Palestine, but with the understanding that in achieving this, nothing should be done to threaten the rights of other people, the Arabs living there, or Jews in other countries."

"That wasn't much of a breakthrough, was it? Just 'viewing with favor,' if the Jews don't cause any disturbance to anyone else?"

"No, you're right. But it's better than nothing, considering the source. It was the joint opinion of the British cabinet at the time. Balfour was Foreign

Secretary. A ray of hope. When Weizmann met with King Faisal, they signed a peace treaty, but that's not very effective either. It's not easy being a Zionist, you see. Let's order lunch, so that we can get back to the hall for the afternoon session. Oh, but we should leave time for dessert, the famous Sacher torte."

"I know a place where the pastries are better," said Elisabeth.

"Then that's where we'll go after the session."

Walking back into Weiner Concert Hall, they met three young men who greeted Nachman like brothers. He introduced them to Elisabeth as David, Shmuel, and Chaim, all of whom had stopped over in Vienna en route from their homes in Russia to Palestine.

"We can't thank you enough, Nachman," said Chaim.

"It's our dream to go to Palestine, and you have made it possible," said David.

"Thank you, thank you," Shmuel said, nearly in tears.

"I suppose it is none of my business," Elisabeth said, as they moved on, "but are you paying for their move to Palestine?"

"My privilege," was all he said in reply.

Late in the afternoon at Elisabeth's favorite Café Central, where politics and pastries vied for priority, the energy of the place was the perfect setting to continue the stimulation of the day and of Nachman's company.

"How long will you be in Vienna?" she asked.

"Just another day, until the end of the Congress. Then I leave for London and sail to New York from Southampton next week."

"All on Zionist business?"

"A little. I will see some of my Zionist friends there—but I still have to work at my business. Since my father died, I have complete responsibility for our operations."

"And what is your business?"

"My company manufactures tires and other heavy rubber goods used in machinery. Since the war, business in Europe has not recovered, but it is booming in the United States. I've made excellent contacts there through my Zionist activities. I will be introduced to new business partners. Also, I want to look into investing in the stock market there. I have already started building a new plant in England."

Elisabeth tentatively asked Nachman how old he was.

"Thirty-one," he said. "Why?"

"You have accomplished so much for such a young man—so many activities all bubbling at the same time. I feel very modest by comparison. Just a lowly art student whose mother is trying daily to marry off, so I can become an opinionated snob like she is."

Nachman laughed heartily. "No, no. You're not like that. You have a lively mind. I won't let you turn into what you think your mother is. I'm spreading out my business for a reason. One can't be too careful, especially a Jew, about, what do they say?—'all your eggs in one basket.' What's going on in Germany now—believe me, that's enough to make me hedge my investments. Building my new house in Warsaw is probably silly, but that's still my home—for now."

"You'd leave Poland?"

"Poland, all of Europe—for Jews these are not havens. There's a guy in Germany, born in Austria, who started a ruckus in a beer hall in Nuremberg two years ago and was sentenced to prison. In prison he wrote a book that's a diatribe against Jews. It just came out last month. Hitler, Adolf Hitler, that's his name."

"So, this is what you meant when you said the Germans would still threaten us, this morning when we read the inscription on the door of the concert hall?"

"Absolutely. I'm no prophet, but this man has followers—not just hooligans like him, but rich friends still seething about how Germany was treated at Versailles. If things don't improve economically in Germany, the people will be up in arms, and this Hitler is just the kind of person to whip them up. Anti-Semitism is the crux of his political philosophy, if you can dignify it by calling it philosophy."

"Even in Vienna, in the little cocoon that my parents think is around us as assimilated Jews, there is anti-Semitism just below the surface of polite society. I heard whispers at the university when I scored a prize, and my brother, who surprised me by attending your congress today, has had the door of his lodging defaced by slogans."

Nachman paid the check and gave Elisabeth his arm as they returned to the street.

"I would have liked to meet your brother. Perhaps another time. Elisabeth, I want to stay in contact. I will be away for several months but I expect to return to Vienna in winter. Please say we'll see each other again."

Her acceptance of his tender hug signaled her answer better than words.

Elisabeth floated home, tingling with excitement from the chaste embrace and marveling at her attraction to the homely man from Warsaw.

Chapter 5

THE FOLLOWING SATURDAY, as Elisabeth was getting ready for her date with Dr. Weinberg, her mother marched into her room without knocking. Elisabeth could always sense a storm on the horizon when her mother barged in. Sitting at her dressing table, she could see in the mirror that this would be no ordinary chat.

"I played bridge this afternoon. . . . "

"Did you win or lose, Mother?"

"It doesn't matter. What is important is what I heard about you from Bertha Friedlander. Who was that man?"

"What man?"

"An ugly little Jew you lunched with at the Sacher the other day."

"An ugly . . . ? How charming. Is that what your friend Bertha said?"

"Bertha is an old and trusted friend, and she has known you since you were a baby. She only has your best interests—and our family's—at heart. She saw you with an unknown gentleman, but that might be too complimentary a description, from what she said. Who was he, Elisabeth?"

"His name is Nachman Tanski, and he's from Warsaw. He might not be Bertha Friedlander's idea of handsome but he's smart, witty, and excellent company. And, Mother, I think he is very rich."

"Well, Bertha said he is very ugly—too Jewish-looking."

"Whatever that means. Bertha, such a beauty herself."

"Well, she was once, before she let herself go and got fat. But don't change the subject, Elisabeth. Where did you meet this Mr. Tanski?"

"At the Art History Museum. In front of a Rembrandt self-portrait."

"A casual meeting at the museum and you end up out to lunch with him, a perfect stranger?"

"We had coffee the day we met, and he invited me out to lunch after that." Mentioning the Zionist Congress would truly lead to bloodshed.

"Well, it is a good thing that you have this invitation from Jack Weinberg, a proper suitor. I won't have you consorting with any old Jew from Warsaw. Do you plan to see this Tanski again?"

"When he returns to Vienna, yes. He is traveling now to America on business."

Mercifully, the doorbell chimed. Elisabeth's mother swept out the door to greet Jack, leaving her daughter aggravated, her face flushed, but grateful for having had the last word.

She convinced herself by the end of the evening that she really ought to have enjoyed Jack Weinberg's company. He must be bright, she thought, to have achieved the academic honors and medical skills that Father bragged about, so why is he so utterly boring?

Not that he was unpleasant. On the contrary, from the moment she had appeared, in diaphanous jade green chiffon, he was the soul of attentiveness and flattery. He seemed sincere enough when he told her how beautiful she looked and how clever her comments were. Elisabeth wished she could say the same about his. His conversation centered on what people were wearing, gossip about a couple who had returned separately from a vacation in the Italian lake district, disdain for the group sitting next to them who, during an intermission, discussed the performance in, horrors, Yiddish.

Perhaps the problem, she figured, was that Jack was not Nachman. Her encounter with Tanski had transformed Elisabeth's ideal of a relationship with a man. While she acknowledged, and could see from the stares from other women in the audience, that Dr. Weinberg was a catch to be envied, she had experienced a man who treated her as an intellectual equal.

This insight struck her just as they entered the Sacher for a post-opera supper, her second meal there in a week. Her escort, awed by the reputation of the legendary hotel and restaurant that he was patronizing for the first time, gushed endlessly about the crowd around them, the "classiness" of the surroundings and menu. But Elisabeth knew how a nice young lady from a nice family behaves with a gentleman escort—you listen politely, smile up at him, appearing to hang on his every word. Nauseating. He probably thinks I adore him, she thought.

Upon returning her home, he ended the evening with his count-like bow and a two-handed grasp of her hands. If he had kissed one, she would have burst out laughing.

"Would you do me the honor of joining me for tennis and a picnic in the country with some friends next Sunday?"

Why not? She loved to play tennis, and summer would soon be over. A day in the country would be pleasant. Not worth it to invite parental reverberations. Accepting this invitation could go a long way toward forging a cease-fire with her mother.

Summer flowed into autumn, and Elisabeth was still seeing Jack, but only once a week. In between, he would be invited to a meal at the Heilbrun home, though on those occasions he spent more time with her father than anyone else. Disappointed that his son, Erich, had chosen the law rather than medicine, Oscar Heilbrun found in Jack a surrogate son who possessed not only the technical skills of a superb surgeon in the making but also the air of superiority ideally suited to a surgeon's ego.

Acceptance by her father gave the young doctor the confidence to stop trying to impress Elisabeth, and she had to admit that the more natural Jack was becoming better company. Still, he was not Nachman, whose letters, though few and infrequent, indicated that his return to Europe would be delayed for several months. To keep the time from dragging, she volunteered with the Zionists—writing newsletter articles, organizing meetings, and arranging lodging and financial support for pioneers coming through Vienna en route to Palestine. She made notes about her activities so she could include updates in her letters to Nachman.

Erich, increasingly consumed by Zionist activities, disliked Jack intensely and rarely came home even for dinner. The senior Heilbruns, content to have the young doctor around, didn't seem to miss their son, which upset Elisabeth. She and her twin made a point of getting together for coffee or lunch every few days, in addition to attending meetings and rallies together. Some were held in Leopoldstadt, and it gave both Heilbrun twins an extra sense of pleasure to be welcomed into homes in the district that their parents considered to be a dreaded ghetto. The local Zionist organization afforded her a new set of friends, which, combined with her studies, made her weekly dates with Jack bearable as just another way of occupying her time until Nachman's return.

Jack did not see their relationship as platonic. Although he remained respectful of what he must have assumed was virginal reluctance, she realized that he wanted a commitment and let him think she was indeed innocent of any other interest in men. Little did she know, however, that she was not the only one keeping a secret. Jack and her parents had decided by October that he and Elisabeth would be betrothed after the New Year. It was not a contractual arrangement, but, when he produced a diamond engagement ring on Saint Valentine's Day, the smug looks on her parents' faces told her that this was no surprise to them and a deal had been struck. She felt like human chattel sold without consent.

When she did not immediately accept Jack's proposal, her astounded parents ranted that she was an ungrateful prig—hypocritical, she thought, coming from them. How could she turn down such a fine young man with so much promise? Who did she think she was?

Gradually, as her health and studies began to suffer from the warfare at home, she broke down and told Jack she would marry him after graduation. By this time she had not heard from Nachman for three months. She began to think that their brief liaison had been just that, and that marrying Jack would blot it out. By the middle of March, a June wedding date was set, and the announcement of Jack's appointment as Dr. Heilbrun's heir apparent as chief of surgery followed a week later.

In late May, just after she had completed her final examinations, Elisabeth and her mother were going over table seating charts for the wedding dinner, a process crucial to Gertrude Heilbrun but of no interest to the bride-to-be. Grateful for the ring of the telephone, she escaped to the hallway and picked it up. It was Nachman, calling from Warsaw, wondering why she had not answered any of his letters since December.

"Letters? What letters?"

She yelled into the phone, as if her screams could be heard all the way to Poland without benefit of the connection. Slumped against the wall, she glanced up at her mother, who, instead of coming out of the dining room to investigate the commotion or comfort her daughter, stood next to the table, her eyes affixed in the opposite direction. In that instant Elisabeth understood what had happened.

The level of emotion that she had poured into resisting Jack's proposal was a mere skirmish compared to the war she waged in the wake of the discovery that her parents had destroyed months' worth of letters from Nachman and also intercepted hers to him. Unrepentant and insisting that they had acted in her best interest, they would not even consider meeting the "ugly Jew" from Warsaw. Erich and his friend, Heinz, spent an entire afternoon vouching for Tanski, an effort that not only proved ineffective but also inadvertently informed the Heilbruns of their children's Zionist involvements, another mark against him.

Elisabeth had two options—defy her parents by canceling her wedding and running off with Nachman, whom, in truth, she did not know very well—or cut her ties with him. In the end she was not strong enough to abandon her family.

Despite the storm that engulfed the Heilbrun household in the month before the wedding, Dr. Jacob Weinberg did not know, as he watched his bride glide down the synagogue aisle toward him, how close he had come to losing her to a man for whom she harbored unrequited passion.

Chapter 6

Eleven years of marriage to Jack produced six miscarriages and Lily. The little girl, at seven, already displayed signs of the curiosity and rebelliousness that had been squelched out of her mother by her union with a man she did not love. Remarkably, in spite of his stiff and stuffy personality, the girl's father indulged her whims and encouraged her independence. While Elisabeth cherished Lily and strove to not replicate her mother's childrearing mistakes, she resented that her daughter favored her father. Eventually, she convinced herself that this was a classic psychological phenomenon, that she was a better mother than her own mother, and that she was the kind of mother Lily would appreciate more when she got older.

Jack's ego and arrogance increased proportionately with his acclaim as a surgeon, and Elisabeth had reason to suspect that his vanity had also led him to be unfaithful to her. Confronted by her suspicions, he actually slapped her and flew out the door in a rage, a scene thankfully not witnessed by Lily, who was at a swimming lesson. The Heilbruns refused to believe anything negative about their precious son-in-law, so their daughter kept her anguish to herself.

Elisabeth's only ally in the family was her twin brother, Erich. He and Nachman had stayed in touch and got together when the Pole came to Vienna. Elisabeth archly refused to join them for several years, until after the scene about Jack's suspected affair. While their relationship remained platonic, which required tremendous willpower on her part, it restored an emotional and intellectual vitality that she had thought she'd lost forever.

Secretly, she had continued her Zionist involvements, along with her brother. When the Nazis came to power in Germany, the movement's urgency intensified.

"I want to move to Palestine," Erich proclaimed one day, drinking wine with his twin sister and Nachman in a Leopoldstadt restaurant after an emergency meeting.

"Mother and Father would die, if you went," said Elisabeth.

"They'll be just fine. Your dear husband is their son now," he said.

Nachman drummed his fingers, saying nothing.

Erich persisted. "Nachman, don't you think it's hopeless here for Jews?"

"How can you even ask? Hitler wants Austria. It's just a matter of time before it could be impossible to leave."

"As it is, there are fewer and fewer places to go," said Elisabeth. "I begged Jack to apply for a residency visa in America when he was invited to speak at a conference in Boston last year. But he simply went on the trip without me and came back. He won't hear of leaving."

"And you're the one saying our parents will die if *I* left the country? What about if you left, with Jack and Lily?" asked Erich. "Tell me the difference."

"We would have taken them with us to the States. But they'd never consider Palestine."

"I don't think they'll ever leave Austria, or even think about it," her brother said.

"Erich, for Palestine, apply now. The British are clamping down on Jewish immigration, but, as a lawyer, you might get in," said Nachman.

"What will happen in Poland, Nachman?" Elisabeth asked. "What are you going to do?"

"My business in London I set up years ago. Warsaw—I have no illusions about. This trip now I'm winding up some loose ends with my Vienna partners, transferring assets to England and New York."

"Soon there will be nowhere to go," Elisabeth said, as she sighed and stood up. "And on that gloomy note, I have to go home. The Seder tomorrow will not get prepared on its own. Six o'clock, you'll arrive? I want to start early, so it won't be too late a night for Lily. Don't drink too much tonight."

Nachman's friendship with Erich made it easy to invite him to the family Seder. The Heilbruns, now frail and increasingly impaired, had forgotten all about the "ugly Jew" from Warsaw who had captured their daughter's heart and almost derailed her marriage eleven years before. Jack had met him once or twice in the past but remained in the dark about his wife's relationship with Tanski. His own outside activities made him oblivious to any longings his wife might have for someone else.

But none of them were prepared for Nachman's entrance that night. He arrived promptly at six carrying a large box, which he presented to Elisabeth with a quick European double-sided kiss of greeting.

"Careful," he said, "it's heavy—and can break."

"Let me put it down on the sideboard to open it. Nachman, I don't know what it is, but. . . ." She opened the package. "Oh, it's magnificent."

"It's a Seder plate. See? I hope you like it," he said.

Even the ailing Heilbruns limped into the foyer to see what Elisabeth had unwrapped. This was no ordinary Seder plate but a masterpiece with three royal blue glass tiers held together by sterling silver, with pearls and sapphires dotted along the silver edges.

Little Lily stood transfixed as the silver gleamed under the light.

"Is it too late to use it tonight, Mama? Can we take everything off the other one?"

"Of course. This is too exquisite not to use, but just sitting here it's beautiful. Helga," calling the maid, "come here, please, and take this into the kitchen. I'll move everything in a minute. What's this?" A small starched booklet had slipped out from the wrappings.

"It's a certificate of provenance," said Nachman. "This is from the sixteenth century—an artist from Venice named Abramo di Salomone."

"Must have cost a fortune," said Jack, still crass, despite all of his claims to refinement.

"Nachman, how can we ever thank you for this gift?" Elisabeth unabashedly flung her arms around him, forgetting for a moment where she was and with whom.

"Here's how you can thank me. Use it in good health for many Seders to come," he said, adding, "God—and Hitler—willing."

That sparked a debate that even roused the old Heilbruns out of their stupor.

"I fought for the Emperor Franz Josef; he awarded me a medal. I operated on him. Me, a Jewish surgeon—I saved the Emperor's life. We are as Austrian as anyone else in this country. We're not going anywhere," said the doctor, "and nothing will happen to us."

Jack agreed. "We are loyal citizens and valuable to the nation. If you mean that we're in jeopardy because we're Jews, I think you're wrong, Nachman."

"I admire your faith, Father and Jack, but it's blind," said Erich. "Do you read the newspapers? Do you know what's happening in Germany?"

Elisabeth decided against plunging into this conversation and said it was time to take a group photograph and then start the Seder. Although she told Lily not to look so scared and to smile for the picture, she knew that Erich and Nachman were right and that her daughter had reason to be frightened.

Chapter 7

THE SEDER RITUAL traditionally ends with "next year in Jerusalem." But Lily's father, Dr. Jacob Weinberg, spent the next Passover in Dachau.

A month earlier, three days after the Anschluss, the German takeover of Austria, a posse of Nazis had invaded the Weinberg apartment and wrenched him from home. The elegant glass and silver Seder plate, displayed prominently in the dining room when not in use, caught the eye of the lead officer, Rudolf Bucholz, who personally carried it out the door.

As Elisabeth presided over a holiday gathering consisting of just her parents, brother, and daughter, she could not help but recall the Seder of the year before in light of everything that had transpired since. Nachman had wound up his Austrian business affairs and no longer traveled to Vienna. She and Erich had said farewell to several Zionist friends lucky and smart enough to exit the country before Hitler took over. Her brother had escaped deportation to Dachau only because he had been working on a case in Amsterdam when the sweep occurred.

Their father was spared, too, but only after the elegant and arrogant old Dr. Heilbrun had been forced onto his hands and knees to scrub the sidewalk outside the university hospital, jeered by onlookers, including non-Jewish medical colleagues and hospital staff. Afterward he was barred from entering the building. Still, he and her mother stubbornly resisted any mention of leaving Austria.

"I'm telling you, it will blow over," the doctor said. "You'll see. The Austrian people and the Germans will rise up and get rid of Hitler, elect someone else."

"Erich," Elisabeth said, "what can we do to convince Mother and Father that it is over for the Jews here?"

Her brother simply shook his head in frustration. He had abandoned his earlier plan to go to Palestine when their mother had suffered a stroke the previous summer. The old woman had recovered all but the use of one arm. Her ability to speak had been left unimpaired.

"You're cowards, you two," she said to her children. "We don't run away from trouble. We're loyal Austrians, we'll be fine. What kind of an example is it to set for Lily if we all just leave, especially while dear Jack is gone?"

Mother always knows how to attack where I am most vulnerable—Lily, Jack's pride and joy—Elisabeth thought. Here I am holding this family together, I am Lily's only visible parent at the moment, and all Mama can do is chastise me for not setting a good example. Leaving would save our lives. Where is the bravery in capitulating to death?

"It's not going to blow over," Erich said. "You think we're some kind of special brand of Jews who will remain immune to what happens to others. Father, you were pushed to your hands and knees and humiliated on the sidewalk. Jack is not away on holiday, he's in a concentration camp, for God's sake. This doesn't convince you that things have changed?" By this time he was screaming.

"Calm down, Erich," said Dr. Heilbrun. "What happened to me was just a bunch of hooligans whipped up about Hitler coming to town. As for Jack, Cousin Hans has already been released from Dachau. I'm sure that Jack will come home soon, too."

Elisabeth said, "But, Father, you've already been barred from the hospital. Jack would be, too. Lily can't go to her school anymore. Every window of shops owned by Jews is defaced, covered with hateful slogans, forbidden to customers. Doesn't that give you some inkling that our future is doomed?"

"Doomed. Such a strong word, my dear," said her father. "We shall not speak of this again."

By the following autumn, neither the Heilbruns' minds had changed nor had Jack returned. On Yom Kippur Erich announced that he had booked passage to Shanghai, one of the few places still open to Jews without visas. He left Vienna the next night.

Early in November Elisabeth received the news, communicated in a telephone call from their district police station, announcing that her husband had died at Dachau of a heart attack. She gasped in shock, letting the phone dangle from its cord when she heard the news. More than any other emotion, she felt disbelief. Jack was only 38 years old and had never exhibited any signs of heart disease. But there was no place to take any inquiries or disputes. His body was not returned.

Even if Elisabeth had chosen to mourn, there was no time.

The next day, November 10, 1938, she and Lily awoke to streets laden with broken glass and the smell of fire permeating the air. The night before was the infamous Kristallnacht, when rampaging Nazis in Germany and Austria destroyed more than 200 synagogues and all businesses owned by Jews.

This time Elisabeth called Nachman for help. He told her that the Nazis were allowing Jewish children to leave through a program called the *Kindertransport*, which would take them to England. Elisabeth's older sister there, Charlotte, and her husband, Arnold, frantic over conditions in Vienna, would provide a safe home for their niece. When she first heard about the plan, Elisabeth demurred. She didn't want to admit to Nachman that she could no longer afford to buy Lily's passage. Sensing this, he arranged on his own for a permit and sent her the ticket for a December 2 departure.

The day before, she started to pack her daughter's clothes.

"Mama," said Lily, "are we going on a trip?"

"You are. You are going to visit Aunt Lottie and Uncle Arnold in London."

"Aren't you coming, too?"

"Not right now, darling. I have to take care of Grandmama and Grandpapa, you know that. They are all alone, except for me, since Uncle Erich left for China. I'll come when I can. Maybe we'll all come."

"Am I going by myself?"

"No, there will be other children with you on the train and the ferry boat. A whole group of children and some nice ladies who will look after you, like teachers."

"Like a school outing. That will be fun." Lily's enthusiasm eased her mother's misgivings only a little. Would she ever see her bright and pretty daughter again?

"And, remember, your Aunt Lottie only has sons, your cousins, Julian and Daniel. She can't wait to have a girl in the house. She'll take you shopping and to the ballet and out to tea. You'll have a wonderful time."

Somehow, she kept up that level of excitement about Lily's departure—and the likely fiction of an early reunion—with both the child and the grandparents. The Heilbruns, of course, disapproved. It didn't matter. Once and for all, Elisabeth was going to assert herself so that at least her child would escape whatever the Nazis had in store for the rest of them. Seeing Lily get on that train was Elisabeth's most painful moment, and her proudest.

An hour after her sister called to say that Lily had arrived safe and sound, a new band of Nazis pushed and shouted their way into Elisabeth's apartment and transported her to a two bedroom flat in Leopoldstadt already inhabited by another family of three. At the same time, her parents were rousted out of their elegant penthouse and delivered to a shabby building in the district they had previously only visited to order new clothes. Now truly a ghetto, for Elisabeth and the Heilbruns it turned out to be the haven of their last days in Vienna.

Elisabeth surprised her parents by managing to forage food and medicine to keep them as nourished and comfortable as possible. Her years with the Zionists had made her a well-known and beloved figure in some quarters of Leopoldstadt. In the course of her work there, she had helped many families or their offspring depart for the relative safety of Palestine supplied with food, medicine, warm clothing, and cash beyond their own means. These activities smoothed her way into the communal life there. Her parents, still insisting that they would be moving home at any time, were only tolerated because of Elisabeth's efforts to pitch in for the good of the community. She even convinced her doctor father to minister to its sick as best possible under the unsanitary and ill-equipped conditions.

Elisabeth sometimes assisted him, giving their relationship a new dimension and vitality after so many strained years. Together they delivered three babies, she tending to the mothers during labor made more arduous than normal by the lack of any anesthesia. When the eleven-year-old son of the Zionist newsletter's editor tried to escape the ghetto to forage for food and broke his ankle running back through the alleyways, Dr. Heilbrun set the bone while regaling the boy with the story of Robinson Crusoe.

Scenes like this astounded Elisabeth, giving her new respect and affection for her father. Infection and disease were rampant, and often no more could be done than simply offering patients comfort and what little palliative potions or pills could be salvaged from supplies they and others had hoarded from the past.

Their makeshift life in Leopoldstadt lasted for almost three years, during which conditions deteriorated sharply. More and more Jews were squeezed into already overcrowded quarters, and food and supplies grew even scarcer.

Elisabeth, who had sent with Lily years' worth of notes, pictures, and news clippings, told herself that she could remain in contact with her daughter through short messages written on whatever small pieces of paper she could find, even though mail service from Leopoldstadt to London was not guaranteed.

One chilly morning, straining to see through a filthy window a few gloriously colored leaves she wanted to describe for her daughter, she witnessed the arrival of a fleet of trucks lining up on the street below. The brusque shouts of *"Juden rost"* and the rhythmic pounding of boots mounting the stairs reached crescendo level outside her door. By that time the screams of neighbors, some with bawling infants, already shoved from their apartments into the hallway contributed to the contrapuntal prelude to Elisabeth's own eviction.

She soon fell into the procession, along with her parents and the other seven people who had shared the space meant for four since the previous winter. Outside, it took all her strength to push her mother up onto the truck before a guard clobbered the infirm old woman with the butt of his rifle. By the time they reached the railroad station, Gertrude Heilbrun no longer spoke, but just stared blankly at her husband as he whispered to her that they would be all right. Elisabeth could no longer argue.

In the boxcar taking them "east," Dr. Heilbrun told his daughter that he was proud of her. Her mother, crushed up against them, silently died. When the railroad car's doors were finally unbolted, her body was cast off like a pail of dung.

A hundred kilometers later the train stopped in the middle of nowhere. Elisabeth, her father, and their fellow passengers were pushed toward a precipice, ordered to undress, and, in groups of one hundred, shot dead and bulldozed into the ravine below.

This happened near Minsk in the autumn of 1941.

PART III

*New York City and
London, March 1990*

Chapter 8

I'm NORMALLY not wakened or annoyed by the hubbub on Central Park South, sixteen stories below. But, as the day after the auction dawned, the bleep of a doorman's whistle to summon a taxi and the scraping of a garbage can being lifted off the sidewalk—a rare and welcome occurrence in New York then—jarred me awake at six-fifteen, after less than five hours of sleep. Just as well, since it was nearly noon in London, and I could reach my daughter at her office. I picked up the phone and dialed London.

"Elizabeth Kovner Aarons," said the voice on the other end.

Elizabeth is an investigative journalist with the *Times of London*. Imagine how gratifying it has been for me that she followed in my professional footsteps, although, as with my son, I would be happier if she lived closer. However, marrying Jonathan Aarons, son of my *Kindertransport* chum, Liesel, was a match that delighted me, even if his career as an investment banker "in the City" mandated that they live in London. Life could be worse—one kid in San Francisco, one in London, and me between them in New York City.

Quickly, I told Elizabeth about the auction.

"You're going to look for that Seder plate, aren't you?"

That's my girl!

"Of course, darling. Even though Uncle went on about the dangers of anything related to ex-Nazis. His exact quote was this would not be 'child's play, like searching for the Afikomen.' So, I've named the quest Afikomen. Clever, huh?"

She laughed. "Yes, Mother, cute. You know, I saw a piece in the *London Jewish Chronicle* last week about a woman who is helping victims of Nazi art looting on a consultation basis. I don't know if I still have it, but my friend, Mark Silver, wrote it. I'll call him."

"Thanks, darling. It would be great to get this woman's name and contact information."

"Look, Mother, I hate to do this, but I have to run to a press conference at the Yard. Let me ring off and try to reach Mark before I leave. I'll call you back later whether I get the information or not. Okay?"

"Fine, dear. Thanks."

By this time it was still not even seven in the morning, too early to make any more progress on Afikomen and, anyway, time for my daily swim. Swimming is not only my favorite form of exercise but also the activity that affords me the best opportunity for concentrated thinking. I like to say that it smoothes me out.

Within twenty minutes, I had fastened on my goggles and plunged into the club pool across the street, alternating crawl and breaststroke for forty minutes, my arms, legs, and breath synchronized in automation. Only my mind floundered. Journalistic fervor—and bravado—aside, how would I go about finding the Seder plate and its mysterious owner? Should I even go further? Did I need to have it? Did I need anything material at all? No.

Was pursuing this worth it? It wouldn't bring back my family. Would it, instead, stir up memories and a sense of loss I tended to gloss over and in the process play havoc with my mental equilibrium? But, as I touched the side to finish my last lap, the positive flow from my swim began to create a plan that could take me to London and Israel, a desirable side benefit. A source like Simon Wiesenthal would prove useful. Simon Rieger? A source? A relationship? That would surely be an unexpected benefit. Nah—better forget that and concentrate on the main event, Afikomen. On its own, enough to tantalize my sense of adventure and my nose for a story. I'd manage to deal with my emotions. I always had.

By the time I got home from the pool, Uncle had left a message saying he had spoken to Wiesenthal, who awaited my call. When the legendary Nazi hunter came on the line, he sounded brusque, but courtly.

"Mrs. Kovner, Nachman Tanski tells me you're interested in Rudolf Bucholz. We've been looking for him since 1945—poof, vanished into thin air."

It surprised me that Bucholz was such a prime target after all these years. "Art looting made him so notorious?"

"Art looting—that was only one of his crimes. Not the worst, by any means. The massacre he perpetrated in Rohatyn—that was something else again."

"Where's Rohatyn?"

"A small city in Galicia. You know where Galicia is?"

"Now the Ukraine, I think. Poland before, and before that the Austro-Hungarian Empire? My father was from Galicia, though he was loathe to admit it."

Wiesenthal laughed. "Why is that?"

"He fancied himself a real Viennese gentleman," I said. "Hitler didn't agree."

"I knew many of that type. Myself, I come from Galicia and make no bones about it."

"Getting back to Bucholz. . . . "

"Bucholz became known as the 'butcher of Rohatyn.' In 1943 a convoy of troops was ambushed there. Bucholz wanted revenge. He ordered and directed a sinister operation—two hundred Jewish men immediately executed by firing squad. Then women and children locked in a synagogue that was set on fire."

Visualizing this horror broke my train of thought. A moment passed before I could even muster another question.

"And Bucholz was never apprehended or prosecuted after the war?"

"No, he vanished. His men said he was on leave in Italy when the war ended. There was one man, a Jew from Rohatyn who'd escaped and thought he saw Bucholz in Rome in 1946, but he wasn't sure."

"To think I thought that looting art was his greatest offense. The man must be a monster."

"He was in good company, believe me," said the old man. "You know I worked with the OSS—the Office of Strategic Services—after the war. There was an OSS group among the Monuments Men, the guys who tracked down art looted by the Nazis. Some of those Monuments Men were curator and art historian types assigned as regular army. The ones attached to the OSS concentrated on searching for the perpetrators. I have a copy of their dossier on Bucholz with some biographical information that could be useful to you. My OSS connection provided me with details about art looting—lists that otherwise are only found in the United States Archives. They've been declassified since the late 1970s. Do you have a fax machine?"

This was a potential treasure trove. I gave Wiesenthal the number and thanked him before setting off to the Mosaica office.

Through the storefront window, I could see from the look on her face that Shira Reznik recognized me and I was not a welcome visitor. However, she responded to my buzzing by admitting me silently. While scanning the gallery space for the Seder plate, I noticed a young man helping a likely customer.

"Can we speak privately?" I asked Reznik.

She beckoned me into a private office in back. Despite the piles of papers, catalogues, and books on the desk and several bookcases, what dominated this windowless space was the black metal door of a vault occupying nearly one entire wall.

"My name is Lily Kovner. You know why I'm here."

She nodded. When she replied, her voice dripped with sarcasm.

"No, I can't imagine why you're here. You don't think you made yourself clear yesterday? That the di Salamone Seder plate belonged to your family. Well, let me tell you once and for all—your accusation is totally unfounded. It casts aspersions on a thirty-year-old business that's nothing, if not ethical. Just who do you think you are?"

"I'm sorry to challenge Mosaica's spotless reputation but I know what I saw. Do you even have a certificate of provenance for the Seder plate?"

"Of course, we do. We'd never sell anything without clear documentation of ownership."

"Then my family's name should be on it. I know that we received a record when my family got it as a gift."

"Then you'd have the certificate, wouldn't you?"

"Gee, somehow the Nazis who ransacked our apartment must have just accidentally picked it up when they stole the Seder plate. Of course, I don't. My mother kept it underneath the Seder plate on a shelf. It had details about the master who created it in Venice and names of previous owners."

"So, you have no real proof that this Seder plate belonged to your family?"

"I told you the Nazis stole the documentation. But I do have notes my mother made . . . "

"In other words, no real proof," she said.

I chose to ignore that. "That vault—is the Seder plate locked up in there?"

"I don't have to tell you one way or the other, but, no, it's not in there."

"Prove it," I said.

"Listen, Ms. Kovner, there is no way I will be held accountable by some lady fantasizing about a valuable Seder plate in her past. It's not here. It's probably back in Israel by now."

"Did Professor Rotan take it back?"

"I think so. I'm not one hundred percent sure. Look," she said, all of a sudden softening up, "I'm not your enemy. But I fail to see how I can help you."

"Well," I said, "I guess I'll have to go to Israel and take this up in Mosaica headquarters with your boss, Mr. Ben-Shuvah."

"Be my guest. But you'll have to stand in line to see him. We're sponsoring a major auction in Tel Aviv in a few weeks, so the office is closed to prepare for that. Eliezer, Mr. Ben-Shuvah, is traveling in Europe visiting sellers there to collect and supervise the shipping of major pieces. You won't be able to reach him for at least a week."

"After fifty-two years, what's a week? Speaking of sellers, do you know who the seller of the Seder plate is?"

"Absolutely not."

She'd never offered me a chair throughout this entire exchange. So, when she opened the office door and swept her arm toward it, her intention was clear.

Frustrated, and dubious about Reznik's credibility, I walked home. Even the unusually warm March day didn't perk me up.

Reaching my building, our weekday doorman, Victor, whose mop of black hair and broad abdomen never looked quite right in the gray uniform and cap, greeted me with his signature, "How's it going Mrs. K?"

"Well, Victor, all right, I guess, though there's something bothering me. By the way, how's your brother the police detective?"

"Louie? Pretty good. We don't get together as much as we used to, you know. We'll all be at my folks' for Easter, you know. Why do you ask, Mrs. K?"

"I went to an auction yesterday and saw something that was stolen from my family by the Nazis many years ago. They took it out of the sale, and I'm just now coming from the auction company. It's not cooperating at all."

"Holy cow! Nazis! That's really something, you know. Good luck, Mrs. K."

By the time I let myself into the apartment, Detective Louie Perelli of the New York Police Department was calling to follow up on the conversation he had just had with his brother, Victor, who'd told him all about my problem. I asked Louie about the vault at Mosaica.

"What do you think? Is there any chance of getting in there with a search warrant, Louie?"

"Not without probable cause. Do you have any proof at all?"

"Just a note my mother left. Also, the person who gave her the Seder plate is still living, here in Manhattan. That's probably it."

"No photograph? Nothing?"

"The auction catalogue has a beautiful color picture."

Suddenly, I remembered something else.

"Please, hang on, Louie. One minute."

I dropped the kitchen phone—portables not yet in vogue—and ran into my study, where the cracked hunter green leather album lay on the desk. I opened to the page where my mother described that Seder night and, affixed to it, was a picture, about three inches square, faded gray, in that mottled 1930s black-and-white way, of our family and Nachman gathered around the end of the table with the Seder plate in front of us. Grim-faced in my new Passover dress I looked up at the Elijah's cup on the top. I picked up the phone again.

"Louie, I do have a picture. Not great, but I think it shows my family with the Seder plate. What do you think about a search warrant?"

"Long shot, but worth a try. Can you get me the photo, the notes, the catalogue, and the name of the person who gave it to your parents? Jeez,

Mrs. K, unfortunately, I don't have time to pick anything up now. Maybe tonight, if you're going to be home?"

"Actually, I do have an engagement tonight. What if I leave all of this in a large envelope with your name on it at the desk downstairs?"

"It's a deal, Mrs. K. I'll get it on my way home. I'll see what I can do, but no promises. Okay?"

Only after hanging up with Louie did I listen to my voicemail. Elizabeth had called to tell me she had spoken to Helen Wolf, the consultant on lost art she had read about, who would be delighted to hear from me. Elizabeth read out the phone number and added that it would be great if I came over to London to meet with Helen Wolf, because it would be nice for her and Jonathan to have me there. Maybe that would happen on the way to Israel. There could be time, if Shira Reznik was telling the truth, since I couldn't see anyone important at Mosaica in Tel Aviv for at least a week.

Hearing the clipped Scottish brogue that answered at Helen Wolf's number made me smile.

"Ms. Wolf?"

"Please call me Helen, my dear. By the way, your daughter sounds like a lovely young woman. Now that we've spoken, I'll have to look for her byline in the *Times*."

"Thank you. Do you have children, Helen?"

"Just one son, Abraham. He lives in Israel."

"So, like mine, far from you. Do you get to see him often?"

"At least twice a year. He comes here on business, and I go there. Now that I'm at this consulting work, perhaps it will take me there more often. My grandchildren are in the army now, so it's harder for them to travel."

My journalistic instinct piqued my curiosity about a husband; my manners told me not to probe further.

"I don't know how much my daughter told you but yesterday I saw a Seder plate stolen by the Nazis that I hadn't seen since 1938. I was at an auction here in New York sponsored by a house called Mosaica. I only went because of a writing assignment. You can imagine my shock. I'd assumed the Seder plate had been destroyed."

"Strangely, such incidents occur more and more lately. I suspect many cases will crop up along with the changes in Eastern Europe. It's but a few months since the Berlin Wall fell. Yet, already new sources have opened up."

The journalist in me resurfaced.

"Please, tell me about your background, Helen."

"I trained at university to be an art curator. Then came the war. I'd finished up some graduate work and secured a very junior position in the government helping museums catalogue and transfer major works to the country before the Blitz and keeping them safely tucked up all during the war. Then I worked with the Monuments Men in Germany. It was thrilling going down to underground caves and salt mines, uncovering hidden vaults, casting about in castles. We found such famous works and then we tried to determine where they'd come from, if their previous owners filed claims. More often than not, they didn't. In those cases art was simply returned to its country of origin, where the national museums took possession."

"And what did you do after that?"

"I assumed that experience would make me a shoo-in for a curator's position somewhere prestigious like the Courtauld Institute. I'd been a postgraduate fellow there after a first-level degree at Cambridge. But being Jewish—and a woman—put that sort of career out of reach. Which was the greater deterrent I can't tell you. Even back home in Glasgow, or Edinburgh, the museums turned me down. So, I taught art history at a girls' school."

"And this new career? The consulting? How long have you been doing this?"

"Four years now. Since I retired from teaching. I'm devoting myself to helping people who still have claims of looted art. It's a welcome return to what I was trained to do—and the clearing up of unfinished business."

"Cambridge? You went to Cambridge? Would this have been in the late 1930s?"

"Yes, my dear. Why?"

"Did you know anyone named Shaul Rotan or Eliezer Ben-Shuvah there?"

Helen hesitated a moment before answering, "I don't recall knowing anyone with those names."

I tried another tack.

"Have you heard of Mosaica, by the way? Based in Tel Aviv?"

She hesitated again. "Vaguely," she said.

Another blind alley. I changed the subject again.

"How do you do your work for your clients looking for looted art?"

"There are lists. The Nazis were nothing if not organized, you know, my dear."

"Yes, quite," I said. "What else?"

She hesitated before answering.

"I don't wish to be rude or unhelpful but I prefer to discuss my work in person. If a client can't meet with me—and some can't for either financial or health reasons—I communicate in writing through the mail. Much safer and more secure that way."

That puzzled me, but I decided to let it go until I met Helen.

"I can come over to England and meet you. When would be convenient?"

"How about next Monday, one week from today? I have to make a quick trip to Zurich this week. I'll be back late Friday. Can we talk Saturday? Do you think you can be in London by then?"

"Yes. I'll plan on it. Thank you."

As I reached for the phone book to find the airline's number, I saw the printout from Simon Wiesenthal in my fax machine. Such a reliable gentleman. As promised, there was an abundance of background information on Rudolf Bucholz.

Bucholz came from Munich. His father was a German financier who had contributed to the rise of the Nazi Party. The mother, an Italian, was the daughter of a physician to Mussolini. A distinguished pedigree in certain circles.

What really caught my eye was the notation that Bucholz earned an art history degree from Cambridge in 1937. He joined the SS later the same year and served in the art looting section in Vienna, Warsaw, Amsterdam, Oslo, and Paris. The Rohatyn massacre occurred during his service on the eastern front, after which he was dispatched to northern Italy. I remembered Wiesenthal saying he was reported by his men to be on leave on V-E Day. There were no known survivors. He was an only child and unmarried. His mother had died in 1935, and his father perished in the bombing of Munich. The possible sighting in Rome in 1946 that Wiesenthal had mentioned was reported by one Josef Drimmer, a Rohatyn survivor who worked in Italy helping displaced Jewish refugees emigrate to Palestine after the war.

Drimmer, I read, thought he saw Bucholz drinking wine with, of all things, a Jew involved in the then illegal immigration activities. Years after telling Wiesenthal about this, Drimmer checked back with the Nazi hunter's operation, but no further trace of Bucholz had ever surfaced. Drimmer had settled in Beersheva, Israel, and died in 1980.

Cambridge. There was a connection, I was sure of it. Suddenly, my meeting with Helen Wolf became as urgent in my mind as another go at Mosaica. I picked up the phone and booked my flight.

Chapter 9

A PINSTRIPE-CLAD Simon Rieger at the bar greeted me when I stepped into Il Vagabondo that evening.

I'd scrounged in my closet to strike a balance of trendy, casual, and class—a red leather Italian jacket and matching sweater I'd picked up at a recent Max Mara sale, black wool pants, and boots. I felt great in this outfit, and Simon signaled his approval with a thumbs-up as I approached.

He leaped off the bar stool and opened his arms like an Italian papa. I had been surprised at the choice of this earthy restaurant, originally a bar and bocce club for locals in this formerly Italian neighborhood in the East Sixties near the river. There were two ways to take this. Either I was not young or stunning enough for Simon to be seen with at the fashionable spots like Le Cirque or 21 or—as I preferred to believe—Il Vagabondo was a place where he was comfortable and he trusted that he didn't have to impress me. That the maître d' called him "Simon, my friend" and the staff knew him by name reinforced my conviction.

Our table, apparently his usual, afforded quiet conversation, despite the hubbub of the place. Once I, too, had a drink and we had clinked glasses to "l'chaim," an antipasto plate loaded with Italian cold cuts, cheese, olives, and caponata simply appeared, followed by a basket full of fried calamari.

Noticing that I didn't immediately dig in, Simon said, "Oh, my God, are you kosher? Here I go and order all this *treyf*, and maybe you don't eat it. I apologize."

I laughed. "No," I said, "I love calamari. Some of the salamis on the antipasto are not my cup of tea, but it's more about the salt than the kashruth. Don't worry: I'll eat my share."

"I'm relieved," he said. "It's wrong to make assumptions. I should have asked you, but they always bring this to my table right away. So, tell me, have you made any progress in finding the Seder plate?"

"I'm embarrassed to admit that I did go up to Mosaica. You were right, of course, it was a wild goose chase—the place was locked up and deserted. I went back this morning and had a row with Shira Reznik, who swears that the Seder plate isn't there. She thinks Rotan took it back to Israel. Not that I trust her. I don't know if you've ever been there, but there's a gigantic vault in the private office behind the showroom. I'm trying to get a search warrant through someone I know in the NYPD. I've code named my hunt Afikomen, so it's a search warrant for the Afikomen."

Simon laughed.

"Afikomen!" he said. "You're a pip, Lily. But, if it turns out that Shira Reznik is telling the truth, then what?"

"I've already made plans to go to London and on to Israel. . . ."

"London?"

"Yes, my daughter lives there. She put me in touch with a woman named Helen Wolf, a consultant who helps track down looted art. I'm meeting her next Monday, then I'll go on to Israel, to Mosaica there."

"I know Helen Wolf."

This floored me so much that I pricked my tongue on the toothpick from which I was nibbling a cocktail olive.

"Ouch," I said. "You do? How?"

"I met her when I was in the Army."

"Were you a Monuments Man? She told me that she worked with them."

"I was only a private, just a lackey assisting the curators, like Helen."

"You must have been very young. How did you get assigned to that unit?"

"I didn't get into the war until after I turned eighteen at the end of 1944. But I had two years of college under my belt, including a couple of art history courses. That was a sufficient credential, by army standards."

The busboy whisked away our appetizer plates in time for the waiter to deliver our salads.

"You were only eighteen?" I asked.

"Right. Just a kid."

"So, what did a lackey do?"

"First, I schlepped," he said. "Insignificant little masterpieces out of caves— Rembrandts, Vermeers, Durers, Giottos."

"Oh, my God. Where were you stationed?"

"I started in Austria with Patton's Third Army. We excavated first at Altaussee in the Alps. That's where Hitler hid the booty he planned to put into his museum in Linz. I was part of a crew that transferred what was there to a collection point in Marburg, Germany. In Marburg I met Helen Wolf. She was one of the curators sorting and comparing what was found to records kept by the Nazis."

"Did you see any Judaica?"

"Not at Marburg or Munich. I was assigned there later. The Judaica was transported to a collection point at Offenbach. I got there a few times, and it was fascinating. Thousands of books and documents, scholarly work from the greatest Jewish academics and philosophers in Europe over centuries. Torahs, silver crowns, menorahs, . . . "

"Seder plates?"

"Seder plates. Even though I wasn't assigned to that section, I know that many things were returned to people who made claims. Other art was, too. Did you ever file a claim for your Seder plate after the war?"

"It never occurred to me," I said. "I was only a teenager. It was hard enough to absorb the news about my parents and grandparents. The aunt and uncle I lived with in London were very protective and generous, so I was well provided for. I never thought about the Seder plate. And I certainly wouldn't have had any concept that it was valuable."

"Hundreds of thousands of works that weren't reclaimed were returned to their countries of origin," said Simon. "Others were pilfered. That was part of my job, too, protecting art from the sticky hands of Allied soldiers."

"Maybe someone took the Seder plate home," I said, "and now is trying to sell it."

"Could be, although at least the Americans caught up with most of their soldiers who helped themselves."

"It must have been very interesting for you at such a young age."

"I loved it," said Simon. "The work with Helen Wolf and the Monuments Men inspired me to train for a curatorial career. My father had other ideas, so I ended up at Wharton. That appealed to his sense of upward social mobility but ultimately proved of little use in operating our particular business. That new term 'networking'—or connections—that's what it's all about in the diamonds and jewelry trade. What does your daughter do in London?"

"She's a journalist."

"Like mother, like daughter! You must be very proud of her."

"Yes, I am very proud of Elizabeth and of her brother, Jacob. He's a pediatric oncologist in San Francisco—and, more importantly, the father of my grandchildren."

"How marvelous! How many, how old?" Who would expect that Simon Rieger would take an interest in the minutiae of my family life? His famous charm, I figured.

"They're twins, a girl and a boy, three years old."

"A two-for!"

"Yes. My mother was a twin; she had a brother."

"Lost in the Holocaust, as well?"

"Not exactly, though lost to the family. My uncle left Vienna for Shanghai in 1938, and we haven't seen or heard from him since. Although most Jews left China by the time that the Communists took over in 1949, he didn't. Apparently, he'd married a Chinese woman, who was pregnant and couldn't leave. After that we heard nothing. What about you? Do you have children?"

"Two, a son and a daughter with Janet, that bitch. Sorry. The divorce is a saga that's played out so much in the press—you undoubtedly know enough. Everyone does."

I nodded. "Where are the kids?"

"Michael's up in New Haven. He'd just as soon have nothing to do with me—his mother has done a number on him. But my money he's willing to accept to finance his life as a perpetual student—law school now, at Yale, no less, after a PhD in physics at MIT. He's not totally estranged, just strained. Spends holidays with Janet, but he occasionally turns up at a wedding or funeral on my side."

"And your daughter?" I asked.

"Jill, I'm happy to report, is a different case altogether. She studied art and design, and I think I'm close to talking her into taking over the business one of these days. She has a flair for it, and she's very personable. Customers love her."

"Are they married?"

"Not yet. I'd love some grandchildren, too, but first things first," he said.

"Tell me about your Judaica collection."

"I collect documents and manuscripts: versions of the Passover Haggadah, the Talmud, original writings of scholars, philosophers, and poets. I've studied texts, too, as I've collected. My favorite period is the golden age of the Sephardic Jews in Spain—Maimonides, called 'the Rambam,' and the poet Yehuda Halevi. I have some originals of both."

"Are you Sephardic? The name Rieger sounds German or Eastern European, certainly Ashkenazic."

"Polish. But my mother's family is Sephardic, though they'd migrated to Rumania. That's where she was born."

By this time, the maître d' himself was pouring a bottle of Barolo, while our waiter placed veal entrées in front of us. As Simon picked up his glass for the tasting sip, he grimaced almost imperceptibly before nodding satisfaction with the wine. After replacing the glass, he used the same right hand to rub his left arm above the elbow.

"Are you all right?"

"Fine. Occasionally, my arm bothers me when the weather changes. It got so warm and humid today—this is one of those days."

"Did you break it?"

"More complicated," he said. "I was in a tank that was crushed and burned."

"A tank? Serving with the Monuments Men?"

"No, later, in Israel's War of Independence."

"Really? I thought your father rushed you back to Wharton."

"Not right away. While I was in Europe, I got involved with Bricha Aliyah Bet, the illegal movement of displaced persons to Palestine. First, I was moonlighting—under the radar. I was still technically in the United States Army. I'd had plenty of opportunity to meet survivors still living in camps after they were supposedly liberated. They were getting married there, having babies. I couldn't believe they could just pick up and try to start normal life after all they'd been through."

"I know. Still in camps with no place to go," I said. "Remarkable and dreadful all at the same time."

"I felt like Moses leading them from Egypt to the Promised Land," said Simon. Talk about ego, huh?"

"It must have been exciting. And dangerous," I said.

"I suppose so, but I didn't think about it at the time. I loved it. I was a kid. The fighting was over. There I was—a soldier just schlepping paintings. Not that I didn't enjoy it. And I learned a lot. But smuggling DPs out of Europe, I finally felt that I was really doing something important. I had my real war in the War of Independence."

"But you didn't stay in Israel," I said.

"Something I sometimes regret," he said. "But I was injured, broken in spirit, and with a broken heart. . . . "

His voice trailed off, and he wiped a tear from his eye and took a bite of veal. I waited for him to speak again.

"I'm sorry," he said, taking a sip of water.

I made a no-problem motion with my hands.

Finally, he recovered.

"My first marriage happened there, unbeknownst to the gossip columnists."

"Really?" I was stunned that Simon Rieger was confiding all this to a near stranger.

"Dahlia was a *sabra* woman straight out of Leon Uris. Gorgeous red-head, a Palmach bomb maker. We got married right after the State was proclaimed in May of 1948. Then in August she was killed by a grenade, just a few hours after she told me she was pregnant. By the time my tank was hit in the Negev in October, I didn't care if I lived or died. And I no longer had the will to argue with my father about coming home."

"Dahlia sounds like the antithesis of Janet."

"My marriage to Janet probably resulted from the tank accident addling my brain, as well as nearly costing me an arm."

"So, you came home to recuperate?"

"Not right away. I couldn't be moved for weeks, let alone make the trip. I didn't get home until January of 1949. By that time my arm was almost healed. I went to Philadelphia for the winter term and stayed in school straight through until I graduated in 1950. Israel remains near to my heart. I have an office in the Diamond Exchange in Tel Aviv and a house on the beach in Herzlia.

"I hate to play Jewish geography," I said, "but do you know the name Koopman in the diamond business?"

"Koopman, of course. They moved from Amsterdam to London before the war, and they're active in Tel Aviv. I remember old Arnold and Pieter Koopman and know Arnold's sons, Julian and Daniel. You know them?"

"Arnold's wife, Lottie, Charlotte, was, still is, my aunt, my mother's sister. They raised me when I got to London on the *Kindertransport*. I never saw my parents past the age of eight. Julian and Daniel are more like older brothers than cousins."

Simon thought a minute, as he wiped the last remnant of osso buco sauce off his plate with a hunk of Italian bread.

"Arnold and Pieter were pioneers in the industrial diamond field during the war. They transformed their business from lackluster jewelry retailing to an international empire. Wonderful people. Very ethical. They made a fortune many times over for themselves and their backer, Nachman Tanski. Do you know him, too?"

"Nachman Tanski? For heaven's sake. I've known him since I was a child. Another surrogate father. I call him Uncle. He was a family friend since before I was born. He gave the Seder plate to my parents."

"Have you told Tanski about the Seder plate at the auction?"

"Of course. I went over to his house last night. He put me in touch with Simon Wiesenthal. I spoke with him this morning."

Simon whistled softly. "Impressive," he said.

"And I'd bet it takes a lot to impress you," I said. Dumb thing to say—why did I?

"Not really. Was Wiesenthal helpful?"

After I summarized the information on Wiesenthal's fax, Simon said, "Bucholz sounds like a classic Nazi thug."

"With a Cambridge education. Like Shaul Rotan, Eliezer Ben-Shuvah from Mosaica, and Helen Wolf. They all got their art history degrees there in the late thirties."

"Really? A Cambridge connection. That could figure into Afikomen. Speaking of which, Afikomen means 'dessert,' you know. How about something to fortify you for your hunt?"

"Trust me, I'm fortified. I just polished off this delicious dinner. Dessert would be superfluous."

"You enjoy what you eat. I like that in a woman."

I couldn't resist. "You do? Really? The women you squire around town look like emaciated models. Not exactly my body image. Plus, I've got a few years on them."

"You women! First of all, your dimensions are just fine—for any age. You're stunning, too. And you've got a mind that's focused on more important concerns than how you look."

If he only knew how much time I'd spent on putting myself together for the evening. . . .

This line of conversation ended with the arrival of an unordered but fortuitously timed plate of cannoli and assorted Italian tea cookies.

"Compliments of the house," said the waiter.

"Look at this," said Simon, "we can hardly insult 'the house' by not eating them. Come on, one of these tiny *amaretti* won't hurt you. Really, I love it that you enjoy food. Obviously, I do, too. I even cook. I bet you do, too."

"Yes. I enjoy cooking. In fact, when you called last night, I was baking cookies to send to my kids—it was therapy. I was too jittery from the day to read or sleep. What's your specialty dish?"

"Gvetch. Do you know what that is?"

"Yes, with eggplant and other vegetables, the Rumanian version of ratatouille or caponata."

"Right. I have all my mother's family recipes."

"So, how come we didn't go downtown to Sammy's Rumanian?"

"When you grow up with the real thing, Sammy's pales," he said. "This is nicer, you must admit. Sammy's can be raucous. Plus, not that I'm such a health nut, but there's something about that syrup container full of schmaltz on the table that turns me off. I always feel my doctor's breathing down my neck sight unseen when I go there."

I laughed and said, "It *is* like opening your veins and mainlining the cholesterol right in."

"Come on," he said as we got up from the table, "let's walk off some of our dinner."

Once outside, Simon reached into his pocket, pulled out a sterling cigarette case—how long had it been since I'd seen one of those?—and opened it to offer me one.

"Not for thirty years." I shook my head for emphasis.

"I know, I know," he said, "but I'm down to one or two a day. Do you mind?"

I frowned. "I do, but, if you must."

He lit up clumsily, considering his disabled left arm.

We strolled west and south toward my building, talking, laughing, watching tourists climb onto the horse-drawn carriages alongside the Plaza and clip-clop off. Smoking aside, I could see how this man attracted women. Charming, interesting, intelligent, lively, and, most seductive of all, a listener who made me feel like the only woman in the world. When he'd finished his cigarette, the touch of his hand and of his good arm sweeping around to my shoulder stirred me in a nearly forgotten way.

"Would you like to come up for a cookie?" I surprised myself by asking.

"I'll take a rain check. I need to get up early for a seven-thirty meeting on Forty-seventh Street."

But then he engulfed me in both arms and kissed me with a passion that I surprised myself by reciprocating. Even with the tobacco odor.

"I'll call you," he said. "It's been a wonderful evening."

He eased me toward the security of Marcus, the evening doorman who had just witnessed an unexpected eyeful, and sauntered away toward the San Remo, the celebrated building on Central Park West where he lived.

Chapter 10

THE NEXT MORNING I awoke charged with both energy and optimism. After my early morning swim, I checked my voicemail to find a message left by Detective Louie Perelli while I was out with Simon the night before. The message said that a Mosaica search warrant request had been filed, pending a judge's approval. Though he cautioned that it was far from a sure thing, the uncertainty added to my after-swim invigoration. Edginess would be more accurate.

Waiting patiently has never been my forte. I had to get out of the house. Maybe I could dig up something useful at the cavernous New York Public Library on Fifth Avenue.

I flipped through the card catalogue and found only one book on looted art, which was solely about Paris. I wound through reel after reel of microfilmed newspapers from the 1940s. There were accounts of the Roberts Commission that established the Monuments Men military divisions in 1943, which was still two years before the end of the war! My stomach curdled. Recovering art was a bigger priority in Washington than rescuing the millions of Jews the Nazis would manage to kill in those two years? The indifference of the State Department and President Roosevelt himself has long been public record, but somehow in hindsight this made it excruciatingly repugnant.

Rolling on to 1945, I could barely make out the grainy plastic images of helmeted officers showing off big pieces of loot. I envisioned Simon down in a cave as part of a human chain passing framed Caravaggios up to the surface. That's the kind of discovery that got the publicity. I didn't read about any efforts to find Seder plates or Torahs to return to their owners. After about 1946 Nazi news reverted to Nuremberg. Usually, I love reading old newspapers, but this dredged up a time I choose to forget. And served no useful purpose for Afikomen.

I went home and dug into my own cave. Obsessed, I reorganized drawers, rearranged closets, laundered bathroom rugs, and packed for a trip still two days away.

At one o'clock I flew downstairs to the mailbox. Rifling through the customary wad of bills, bulletins, and solicitations, I flipped to a white business envelope, hand-addressed with no return address. Inside, lined notebook paper bore a message in pasted letters cut from books and newspapers:

Stop your hunt Mrs. Kovner before you get hurt.

This wasn't funny, and I knew from experience it shouldn't be ignored, so I called Louie at the police station.

"I thought such a crudely put-together threat like this only showed up in movies," I said, when he arrived twenty minutes later.

Louie looked up from the letter and said, "Sorry to disillusion you, Mrs. K, but, believe me, y'don't want to know how often we see this junk."

Louie, shorter and built like a bull compared to his brother, had the same mop of black curly hair. Al Pacino he wasn't, despite the black leather jacket and jeans uniform typical of plainclothes cops in both cinema and real life. As he spent a quiet few moments looking around my admittedly affluent, though not ostentatious, place overlooking Central Park, he scanned the paintings and *objets d'art* acquired over the years. I knew what was on his mind.

"You're wondering why I would pursue this, aren't you, Louie?"

He seemed almost relieved.

"Forgive me, but yeah. Y'know, Mrs. K, I saw the picture and the write-up in that catalogue. I know the Seder plate you're looking for must be very special and all, but you've got here this threat and everything"—his hands and eyes gestured slightly around the room—"do y'think it's worth it?"

"I understand your question. You're right. I don't need any material things. But the Nazis stole our Seder plate. They killed my family, and now someone else is trying to make money off that whole horrible series of events. I know it won't bring back my parents. But reclaiming a small piece of my family history and legacy would bring some justice for part of the crime."

"But, Mrs. K, this threatening letter . . . "

"Come on, Louie. When I was working full-time, I published exposés on some pretty tough characters. Do you think this is the first threatening letter I've had in my life? This one looks like an amateur job. I have been stalked by goons on the street and hissed at on the phone. Once, my husband hired an armed security guard to tail me everywhere until I insisted that it would ruin my professional credibility."

At that moment Louie's pager beeped, alerting him to call the station.

When he hung up, he said, "Well, that was my captain. The search warrant has been approved. Seems the judge's mother-in-law is a Holocaust survivor. We'll do it. Eleven o'clock tomorrow morning."

"Can I come?"

"No," he said, "Not a good idea at all. I'll call you as soon as it's over, I promise. But, look, Mrs. K, if y'won't give up, at least be careful. I understand your reasons, I suppose. The threats from before—at least you could figure out who they were. This time you've got no idea who you're dealing with. This may look like scraps some kid put together, but it's not."

I must have taken Louie seriously, because my positive energy dissipated as soon as he left. When the phone rang about seven that evening, I was sight-reading my way through an easy-version piano arrangement of "I Have Dreamed" from Rodgers and Hammerstein's "The King and I."

"Aren't you leaving the day after tomorrow?"

Uncle's habit of launching a phone conversation without salutation was legendary.

"Yes," I said, trying to sound nonchalant, "unless the search warrant at Mosaica turns up the Seder plate."

This news I could comfortably relay. There was no way I was going to mention the threatening letter to a ninety-six-year-old, even one as sharp and pragmatic as Uncle.

"Then plan on dinner with me tomorrow night. The Russian Tea Room at seven."

With my next caller I felt more secure about discussing the threatening letter.

"That's terrible," said Simon. "Are you sure it's safe to be alone? I can come right over."

"I appreciate the offer but I have things to do and I don't frighten easily.

Besides, my police contact, who's already come over, is the doorman's brother."

"Then how about dinner tomorrow, especially if you're leaving town on Thursday?"

"Sure, if you don't mind joining me and Uncle Nachman Tanski at the Russian Tea Room."

So, the going away dinner turned into a threesome, a scenario that thrilled Uncle, a closet matchmaker for everyone but himself. By the time Simon and I approached the regular Tanski booth the next evening, I had almost forgotten about Louie's noontime call reporting the disappointing though predictably negative result of the Mosaica search warrant.

With a huge smile on his face, Uncle popped off the banquette seat like a forty-year-old and embraced the two of us in a three-way bear hug.

"Lily, Simon, what a pleasure!"

"Thank you so much for including me, Nachman," said Simon. "I didn't mean to intrude on your evening with Lily. She's just told me how long you've known each other and how close you two are."

"Nonsense. I was happy to hear that the two of you have met. You and I go back a way, don't we, Simon? The Jewish Museum board—how long ago?"

"I finished ten years on the board last year. It was enough. I think you went off, what, maybe five years before?"

"Something like that. Yes, it was more than enough. I'm way too old for such nonsense. Sitting in board meetings is the last thing I need to waste my time on."

Uncle was really in his element in the Russian Tea Room. Though you'd never call him a show-off, he loved the "in" spots where one would see and be seen. And he loved the food at the Russian Tea Room. By the time we arrived, blinis with caviar and sour cream had already been ordered, and he had emptied a shot glass of vodka.

"L'chaim," said my date, clinking his glass with mine and Uncle's, refilled.

At that moment Shira Reznik, with another woman and a man, walked toward our table, led by the maître d'. Scanning our booth, she frowned when she saw me in the middle, but instantly turned on a grin, stopped, and held out her hands to Uncle on one end and Simon on the other.

"Mr. Tanski, Mr. Rieger," she said, "how nice to see you both."

Gushing. Sickening.

Simon half stood up and said, "Thank you. You, too," then sat down again. Uncle stayed seated and merely nodded. Shira and her party moved on to their less prominent table.

Perplexed, I turned to Uncle. "Do you know her? She's the head of the Mosaica office. I thought you'd barely heard of the auction house," I said.

"I think she used to work somewhere else," he said. "Over the years you see people around."

I let it pass, and he readily changed the subject to my trip. Who was this woman in London I planned to meet?

Simon jumped in and talked about working with Helen Wolf and the Monuments Men after the war.

"That work probably led to my own collecting," he said. "Of course, you were way ahead of me, Nachman. Did you ever retrieve any of what you lost from your Warsaw house?"

"Never," said Uncle. "Not a single thing. I had to start completely from scratch when I came to New York. 1940. You can imagine the bargains then. Here—and in Europe after the war.

"Really? I would have thought Judaica would have been hard to come by for a while," said Simon.

"Somewhere there was always something. A piece here, a piece there. When I was active, I'd accumulate, then auction off, buy more. Like a game. But a younger man's game. Or woman's. Like our Lily here. Maybe, if she finds that Seder plate, she'll pick up a taste for the thrill of the market, too. Buying and selling. What you think, my dear?"

"Afikomen is a matter of family memory. I'm not interested in buying and selling," I said, unaccountably irritated by this strain of conversation.

The waiter couldn't have arrived at a better time to take our order. Uncle's choice of entrée, beef stroganoff, would have put his doctor into cardiac arrest.

Reading my mind when the waiter left, he said, "I'm ninety-six years old, for heaven's sake. It's not like I can die young anymore, right, Simon?"

Simon nodded but changed the subject.

"Do you still get to Israel, Nachman?"

"Absolutely. I spent two months at my home in Caesarea this winter. I love it there. Palm Beach doesn't interest me. Everyone else in New York can have it. How about you?"

"I have a place in Herzlia."

"Almost neighbors. Just down the coast. Lily has a flat in Jerusalem and one in London, so she can take this trip and not even have to check into a hotel."

Now *I* changed the subject.

"Uncle, I told Simon how helpful you were in getting me in touch with Simon Wiesenthal. I'm not sure how useful the bio he sent on Bucholz will be, but maybe Helen Wolf will be able to fill in some blanks. I think she has some lists of Nazi loot."

"Have you found anything else?" Simon asked.

"Yesterday I went to the Public Library. There's microfiche there of old newspaper reports about the discovery of loot. What you told me the other night was more helpful. There *was* a book on art from Paris. Nothing on stolen Judaica or anything about looting in Austria."

"No surprise there. Austria cried victim for years," said Uncle. "Those bastards who welcomed Hitler to Vienna with open arms. Only when it came out about what's his name? The guy who was at the UN?"

"Kurt Waldheim," I said.

"Right, Waldheim. Only since it came out he was a Nazi, finally in Austria they're shamed into admitting a little responsibility. But still it didn't stop them from making him president."

"Have you ever gone back to Vienna, Lily?" Simon asked.

"Once. Arthur had a conference there about fifteen years ago, and we took the kids. It amazes me that Simon Wiesenthal can live there. I couldn't wait to leave."

"Good thing he could give you information on the phone," said Uncle, scraping the last morsel of stroganoff from his plate. "Let's see what they have for dessert."

"Uncle! Enough already. Besides, I really should get home and finish packing."

"Let's get the check," said Simon.

"No need," said Uncle, which meant that he'd arranged to charge on his account before we arrived.

When Simon protested, he waved his hand and said, "The pleasure of an old man. I'm delighted to bump into you again, Simon. And to see you with my Lily."

Taking me into his arms outside on 57th Street, he whispered, "Please be careful, my dear."

Letting me go, he looked back to the door of the restaurant; following his gaze, I turned around and saw Shira Reznik come out just in time to witness this farewell scene. Uncle nodded his head in her direction before he blew me a kiss and got into a taxi. She stood on the sidewalk and watched as Simon took my hand and we began to walk west toward Seventh Avenue. Perhaps it was my imagination or just wishful thinking, but the look on her face told me that not only was I a problem for her, but the company I kept would make me harder to dismiss.

"Well," I said to Simon, "now that you've heard what a real estate magnate I am, would you like to come up and see my digs?"

"Well, maybe just for a little while. After all, you're leaving tomorrow."

"Not until five in the afternoon."

"With Nachman you seemed in a hurry to get home. I thought the two of you were so close," said Simon.

"We are. I just didn't want to forget myself and mention the threatening letter. It would worry him, and he'd press me to give up. Thanks for not saying anything."

"Well, I'm worried. I'm glad you showed it to your friend at the NYPD."

"I'll be fine," I said. "Tell me, what were you getting at about Uncle's looted art? Did you ever hear of anything of his from Poland when you were working in Europe?"

"No. I was just amazed that he could re-amass such a collection so soon after abandoning it all in Warsaw. Did you know that there was an auction from his Judaica collection in 1951, only six years after the war ended?"

"No. In 1951 I was still in England at university. How do you know this, Simon?"

"From the auction's catalogue—it was Park Bernet. He'd sold a manuscript I bought later. I'd seen his name and the date on its provenance document and found the catalogue at the Public Library. I was curious about what else he'd sold then."

"Why would it be strange to have collected so much by then? He said the market was plentiful."

"No reason, probably," Simon said. "I'm a little jaundiced by the Monuments Men experience, I guess. If he never had anything from his Warsaw house returned to him, it's odd to have accumulated enough so soon after the war to warrant an auction. Of course, I didn't really get into the market until much later. I'm just speculating with absolutely no right or reason to question how he did it."

"Was the manuscript's provenance clear from before Uncle?"

"Yes, it listed his purchase from the previous owner in 1942 or 43. Let's forget it. I've never heard any whiff of doubt about Nachman's ethics. Really."

By this time we were in my apartment. I flipped on the lights, and he reacted appreciatively.

"Stunning! Not that I would have expected anything less," he said, taking in my living room. "The artwork is particularly interesting."

I took this as a compliment.

"Arthur and I bought what we liked, mainly on trips, to remind us of good times and places we enjoyed together."

I busied myself putting on a string quartet—Prokofiev, maintaining the evening's Russian theme.

"I remember," said Simon, staring at a photo of my tall, trim, and handsome husband and me on the piano, "that Arthur looked like a cross between Robert Redford and Alan Alda. Tall, lean, athletic, that reddish blonde hair. What a gorgeous couple! You miss him a lot, don't you? Of course, you do. What a stupid question. I apologize."

He turned around and grabbed onto my hand.

Simon may not have been the most attractive man I have ever known, but he was proving to be a stimulating one. Feeling that I was blushing like crazy, I edged back a little and said, "How about a drink, or some coffee or tea?"

"After all that vodka, I shouldn't," he said, "but, if you have anything like cognac, I guess I'd take a little."

Pouring us a couple of snifters gave me time to compose myself and him a chance to peruse my home a little further, including to check out the hallway lined with shelves of books and records.

"Nice music, the Prokofiev," he said, "but do you ever listen to jazz? You have some great stuff here—early Dizzy Gillespie, Gerry Mulligan."

"Sometimes. Those were Arthur's. Put one on, if you want," I said.

"Not now. Your selection's just fine." Taking his glass from me as we sat down on the sofa, he toasted, "To Afikomen and its lovely lady sleuth. Safe travels. Be careful. Please."

"I'll be fine," I said, though I liked that he cared.

"Look," he said, pointing to the left side of my view, "you can see the lights of my building all the way down Central Park West. We could almost wave to each other. Ah, New York. Who knew that living so close to me is this fabulous woman who lives in this gorgeous apartment in which she actually bakes cookies?"

"I don't know why that amazes you," I said, "when the famous man about town, Simon Rieger, brags about making Rumanian gvetch."

"Okay. Point taken."

And then it was me that was taken—into his arms—for a deep kiss that lasted several minutes during which necks, shoulders, and backs were gently caressed. Taking a momentary breath, we straightened up and fastened on each other's eyes.

I spoke first. "I am glad you're here, but. . . . "

Simon sensed my thinking. "You're leaving tomorrow and you have a lot on your mind. Timing is everything, especially when it's right."

It was only after he left that I realized he hadn't had a cigarette after dinner.

PART IV

London, 1990

Chapter 11

I USUALLY VISITED London five or six times a year. I hadn't lived there for nearly forty years, but every trip was a homecoming. While some neighborhoods remained as familiar as my daily haunts in Manhattan, others were prime for discovery. There was always a bookshop I had forgotten or a mews or lane to explore.

London still felt like home, because it had once welcomed me with open arms after Vienna, for which I harbor no loyalty, had cast me out. I had arrived for the first time shortly before my ninth birthday.

I had picked up a few English words as a child in Vienna and, possessed of a good ear, I adapted quickly to the language and curriculum in my new school. My traveling pal, who was now my daughter's mother-in-law, Liesel, attended the same school. We were somewhat of a novelty at first. The school was known to be quite exclusive, especially when it came to Jews, but we donned our uniforms and marched in every day like we were the two royal princesses, not wholly oblivious to our oddity status but determined to blend in.

Two princesses who had traveled to England in coats adorned with yellow Stars of David, both of us booted out of our Austrian schools for months. Just going to school again made us feel that we were accepted. In less than a year we shed the last vestiges of our accents to such a degree that anyone would have been hard put to detect that we were nonnative speakers.

As I didn't leave Britain until my twenties, it was a different story in the States. Even after nearly forty years people occasionally inquire if I came from England—or South Africa or Australia. Hard as I've tried, I still sometimes "fancy a hamburger" or make plans to go to the "cinema." Yet, in London people laugh at me for asking directions to the "ladies room" or departing for the "subway." I am a polyglot within a single language I call greater English.

What I love about England are the trappings—the history, the old news-reel feel of the cabs, the elegant stuffiness of it all. As a Jewish girl growing up during the blight of the war and its interminably shabby aftermath, I hardly lived the life of a Mayfair debutante curtsying at Court to launch the "season" of tea parties, balls, and country weekends. However, I lapped up newspaper accounts of that existence with some envy.

I aligned myself especially with Princess Margaret Rose. When the princesses broadcast to the nation's young people, I took her perky, "Good night, children," as personally as if Margaret had sat across the aisle from me on the *Kindertransport* train. We were the same age, and our mothers had the same name. Of course, Margaret's was the Queen, while mine had been murdered by the time I was eleven, although I didn't know it until five years later.

Despite my contentment in the new surroundings, I resented being sent away when I read that the King and Queen, dutifully traipsing around Blitzed London to lift spirits and reinforce backbones, chose to keep their daughters at home, even after theirs—Buckingham Palace—was bombed. In the end, though, my life turned out to be happier and more fulfilled than Margaret's.

The nadir of my time in London was the summer of 1945, when I rushed out of the cinema, mortified by the first newsreel shots of the liberated con-centration camps. I didn't even stay for the feature, *Blithe Spirit*. For weeks afterward I cocooned in my bedroom, shades down, staring through tears at the four walls, occasionally cracking open some appropriately dismal book like Conrad's *Heart of Darkness*, assigned to be read before the next school term. I emerged at dinnertime when Uncle Arnold came home and reported on his daily trip to the Jewish organization posting survivor lists.

London is also where "Uncle" first became "Uncle." Though he moved on to New York in 1940, he managed to get across the Atlantic often throughout the war and afterward. Well connected through his years of Zionist activities and unlikely, for a Jew, affiliation with the Polish govern-ment-in-exile, he pulled every string and called in every marker to ultimately unearth, in early 1946, information about when and how my mother and grandparents perished.

After my overnight flight, I was well into my London routine by dusk on Friday. With my English cousins I own a compact Chesham Place flat in lovely Belgravia. Their wives furnished it with a fair amount of chintz—not my taste but comfortable and homey in a divine location. I'd arrived there by ten-thirty in the morning, unpacked, and gone for a swim at the nearby hotel pool where I had a long-standing arrangement.

Refreshed and convinced that I'd warded off jet lag, I stopped by the greengrocer's for a few provisions, then came back and sat down on the blue print sofa with a book. When the phone rang at six o'clock, I assumed it was Elizabeth informing me that she and Jonathan would be late.

"We've warned you, Mrs. Kovner, and we mean it—stop your search," said the raspy female voice on the other end.

I stared at the phone in disbelief when the caller clicked off. Who was after me? How could they know where I was? How serious were these threats?

Ten minutes later my daughter, Elizabeth, and her husband, Jonathan, walked in and asked me why I was so pale.

"Just a little tired from the flight," I mumbled.

I perked up when they sat down on the sofa holding hands, so obviously in love. And, I might be biased, but they're a stunning couple to begin with. Elizabeth is the female version of her father with Arthur's light complexion, a mane of wavy strawberry blonde hair, and height of five feet ten, an attribute she only began to appreciate at the age of 16, when the boys caught up. Jonathan, a lanky six feet two or three, like her father, looks just right next to her. My son, Jacob, on the other hand, is a clone of my family with olive skin and dark hair. He stands eyeball to eyeball with his younger sister, an annoyance he got over by the time he went to medical school.

The kids started bubbling about their jobs as I made drinks and set out some cheese and crackers. Elizabeth was working the metro crime beat at the paper and getting a real education on the British legal system. Jonathan's firm in the City had a host of IPOs coming—specifics all confidential, of course—but he thrived on the pace.

I thought I was holding myself together, but my face must have said otherwise, because Elizabeth asked again, "Mother, are you sure you're all right?"

"Well, to be honest, since I began Afikomen, searching for the Seder plate, I had a threatening letter in New York and a phone call here—just a minute or so before you came. Someone doesn't want me to do this."

"An understatement, if ever I heard one," said my son-in-law. "I say, Elizabeth, we need to ring up one of your friends at the Yard."

Elizabeth had already jumped off the sofa and moved toward the phone, fumbling in her bag for a small notebook.

"Sarah Cooks, please," she said after dialing a number. On hold, she turned to me and asked, "Mom, did you call the police in New York?"

"Yes. Louie Perelli. You know Victor the doorman—his brother. He also arranged for the search warrant at Mosaica that turned up nothing."

She nodded. "Sarah—Eizabeth Kovner Aarons of the *Times* here. Fine . . . and you? Listen, my mother's here from New York on a hunt for something that was stolen from her home by the Nazis 52 years ago. She's only just arrived today and she's had a threatening phone call. Yes . . . that's right . . . just now. Also a threatening letter before she left New York."

She handed me the phone. The crisp voice on the other end introduced herself as Chief Inspector Sarah Cooks.

"If you don't mind, ma'am," she said, "I'd like to know something about what you're doing. This search Elizabeth mentioned?"

"When the Nazis invaded my family's home in Vienna in 1938, they took a Passover Seder plate—a very elegant and valuable antique, and I never saw it again until this past Sunday at an auction in New York. It vanished again, after the auctioneers quickly withdrew it from the block when I made a fuss."

"And why are you in London? Do you think it's here?"

"No, but there's a woman I've heard about who helps trace looted Nazi art who's here. I'm going to see her on Monday. Her name's Helen Wolf."

"I see," said Chief Inspector Cooks. "And the threat? You got a phone call? When precisely?"

"About a half-hour ago. A woman, with an accent I couldn't place, said to stop my search. I got a threatening letter in New York before I left. Elizabeth told you that. I was in touch with the police there, too."

"There is not much I can do at this point, sorry to say," she said, "but I'll give you my private phone number. Do call me at any hour, if another call comes in or something else happens. In the meantime, do be careful, Mrs. Kovner."

"Well," I said, after we rang off, "come on, kids, let's go have dinner. There's nothing she can do, and I'm sure these are idle threats, some kind of prank. We have a lot of catching up to do."

The Spanish restaurant, an easy walk from the flat, seemed to be a favorite with the locals, especially the young set, and my daughter and son-in-law greeted and introduced me to a few acquaintances there, including two couples with babies. Elizabeth and Jonathan had been married nearly five years, and I knew that they were trying to conceive. It was a topic I could discuss with Elizabeth privately but not bring up with the two of them, unless they mentioned it, which they didn't. Seeing them with these friends' babies made me wistful about what good parents they would be.

But I couldn't worry about everything, at least not all at the same time.

Chapter 12

WHEN WE SPOKE on the phone, Helen Wolf had invited me to lunch at her flat on Monday.

"It will be a private place to talk," she said. "And I can spread out the materials I have to show you."

The conversation heightened my anticipation of this meeting. As Monday dawned I charged out to the pool with more than my usual vigor, as if this were the first day of a fresh school term. But to get soaked, I hardly needed to swim. The moment I walked out of my building, the sky disgorged a downpour that persisted all morning.

Back in my flat about ten o'clock, I phoned Helen to confirm our noon appointment and to warn her that the weather might delay me. Though I left my flat with ample time, the three-block walk to the Tube station looked like a wade across the Channel, and I settled myself into the empty taxi that had thankfully slowed when I reached the corner. However, its crawl through streets overflowing with both water and traffic did, in fact, make me about twenty minutes late.

Helen lived in the middle of a row of almost identical Edwardian attached white buildings on a side street in Kensington near the Royal Albert Hall. She had told me that her flat was on the first floor.

"Simply ring, and I shall buzz you into the front entrance," she'd said.

Just as I pressed the button under Helen's nameplate, the front door opened, and a tall, blonde woman—dressed, like everyone that day, in a nondescript mackintosh, but with a poplin rain hat poised rakishly over her left eye, à la Marlene Dietrich—stepped out and held the door for me with one hand while gripping a shabby brown leather briefcase in the other.

"Thank you," I said.

Inside the narrow foyer, opposite the stairway leading up to the other two flats, was Helen's door, which I pushed open with a light knock.

"Miss Wolf? Helen? It's Lily Kovner. The door was open. I don't want you to be alarmed."

Other than Brahms's Second Symphony, I heard nothing. I crept along the parquet floor through a narrow foyer, past the entrance to a galley-shaped kitchen into a living and dining room space that defied any stereotype of an old lady's bed-sit in both size and décor—a forest green Danish modern sofa, black leather Knoll arm chairs, Moroccan area rugs, Charles Rennie Mackintosh wooden tables, a few modern paintings on the wall.

The music came from a stereo in a three-sided nook adjacent to the main seating area. A dying fire on a stone hearth was the only gap in the ceiling-to-floor bookshelves that lined each wall. A tidy rectangular Rennie Mackintosh desk and chair faced the fireplace. A puddle of broken glass sparkled on the rug next to the desk.

"Helen? Helen?"

Turning around toward an opening that framed a short hallway on the opposite side of the living room, I saw the soles of two black oxford shoes. Pointing outward like an upside down ballet first position, they were attached to the feet of the inert body of a bald woman sprawled face down on the floor. A gray wig styled in a short bob lay a few inches beyond, in the doorway of a tiled bathroom. I gasped and kneeled down, felt one wrist for a pulse, and realized that I had just discovered a corpse.

I quickly stood up and spun around, listening intently for any sound. Was there anyone else in the flat? Was this Helen? Had she fallen by accident? Or suffered a fatal stroke or heart attack?

Now what?

I found a phone on the bedroom nightstand. What was the emergency number in London? For a minute I just stood there in a daze, receiver in hand, before finally dialing 999 to request an ambulance.

"What's the problem?" the operator asked.

"A woman is . . . .sick," I muttered. "Please send an ambulance. Quickly."

I gave the address and returned to where Helen lay. Next to the wig, I noticed a sheaf of white papers just beyond her outstretched left hand. I crouched down and quickly scanning the one on top—a typed listing of paintings by Picasso and Chagall under the heading VIENNA, 1938. I shuffled through the other pages, all similarly columned with artists' names and titles, until a creased black-and-white glossy snapshot fell out of the pile.

It was a picture of three young adults, two men and a woman, posed on a broad lawn with a round fountain and large building in the hazy background. One of the men was short, dark, and stocky. Even dressed in slouchy trousers and a pullover, not his SS uniform, I recognized him as Rudolf Bucholz, the man who stole our Seder plate that night in Vienna. The other one, taller and fair, could easily have been Shaul Rotan. The woman? Helen Wolf?

Just then the piercing "ee-aw, ee-aw" native to European emergency vehicles—and the Gestapo—wailed up the street and stopped in a screech of brakes. I dropped the photo into my bag, which had remained on my shoulder. Within seconds a two-man crew rolled a stretcher into the flat. I led the attendants to Helen, babbling that I'd arrived for lunch with Miss Wolf and found her like this.

"She's dead," one of the young men said after about a half-minute of checking her vital signs. "Might have 'ad a 'art attack or something like that. Are you the next of kin?"

"Oh, no, I was just coming for a visit. She was expecting me."

As I spoke, I glanced over to the dining table and noticed for the first time that it was set with two places.

"We were going to have lunch. See, the table is even set."

"Hmm. Well, the police will arrive presently, ma'am. Procedure, you know. You must stay put. Does she have anyone, any family that you know of?"

"A son, she mentioned. In Israel. Look, I didn't know her. We'd only spoken on the phone. We were going to meet for the first time today, actually," I said.

"And she invited you to lunch? Never met you before?"

"She said it would be the best place for our meeting."

"Good afternoon. I am Inspector Paul Tarrant," said a tall, trench-coated newcomer, flanked by two constables. "And you are?"

"My name is Lily Kovner. I'm an American citizen. I was invited to lunch by Miss Wolf, Helen Wolf, who lives—lived—here and I arrived to find her—I guess this is Miss Wolf—over there, like that," I said, motioning to the hallway.

"How did you get into the flat? Did she respond when you rang the buzzer outside?"

"No, Inspector. Another woman was just leaving when I came up, and she held the door as I walked in. The door to the flat was ajar and easily pushed open when I began to knock."

"An elderly woman living alone with her door unlocked? A bit unusual, don't you think?" he asked.

"I suppose so, but she was expecting me. You see," I said nodding toward the table, "she'd set for lunch for the two of us."

"Were you two friends or relatives?'

"No, I made an appointment with her last week before I left New York. We spoke again over the weekend, after I arrived in London, and again just this morning. I told her I might be a bit late—with this weather," I said, conscious that I needed to appear sincere and confident, rather than the anxious nervous wreck I was.

"And why did you come to meet this Miss Wolf?"

"She is—was—a consultant to people who had works of art looted by the Nazis during the war and are trying to track them down. I recently learned that something my family owned and had stolen is in the hands of an anonymous collector."

"You don't sound like someone who came out of the Holocaust, ma'am. You sound like a cross between a Londoner and a New Yorker, if I may say so."

"I came here from Vienna when I was eight years old to live with my aunt and uncle. Later I went to the States. My late husband was American, and I have lived in New York since 1954. You have a remarkable ear, Inspector." A little flattery might get me somewhere—out of there, I hoped.

He blushed slightly and softened the timbre, as well as the suspiciousness, of his grilling. "So, you don't even really know that this is Helen Wolf, the occupant of this flat, do you, Mrs. Kovner?"

"That's right, Inspector. I assume that this is Helen Wolf, the resident of this flat. When I was phoning 999, I did see some photographs in the bedroom that seem to be this woman with other people."

"And how long after you arrived did you ring for the ambulance?"

What was the point of asking this? Did he think Helen was murdered? And I did it? Panic was setting in.

"Sir, I found her like this as soon as I arrived, I checked her pulse, and immediately looked for the phone. Why is there suspicion? I was trying to do the right thing, Inspector," I said, as calmly as possible.

"Of course, you were, Mrs. Kovner. No one is accusing you of anything. We simply have to look at any sudden death in a home as a potential case for the coroner until we have a postmortem exam to determine the cause of death. Just procedure, ma'am," he said, trying to sound reassuring.

I exhaled audibly and ventured to ask if I could leave. "I'm quite shaken, as you can imagine."

"If you would wait just a few minutes more, I'd very much appreciate it. Then I can have one of my men drive you to your hotel. Where are you staying?"

"Actually, I am part-owner, with my cousins, of a flat in Chesham Place. I stay there when I come to London."

"Do you come often?" Why did it matter? Would the questions never cease?

"Several times a year. In addition to cousins and friends, my daughter and son-in-law live here; he is English. My daughter's a journalist. On the metropolitan desk at the *Times of London*—crime beat."

"The *Times*, eh?"

"Yes. In fact," I said, fumbling in my bag to find the small slip of paper without pulling out the photo, "she's put me in touch with Chief Inspector Sarah Cooks. I have her private number. Here."

"Thank you." Tarrant looked at the paper and gave it to one of his assistants, instructing him to get Cooks on the line.

"And why would your daughter have thought you might be needing Chief Inspector Cooks?"

"I've had some threats," I muttered.

"Threats?"

"Chief Inspector Cooks, sir," said the voice in the bedroom. Tarrant took the phone, and I heard his laconic side of the conversation, a series of "yes," "I see," "very good, ma'am."

Tarrant hung up and returned to the hallway to supervise the ambulance attendants executing the departure of Helen's body. He didn't say anything to me about what Chief Inspector Cooks had said but supervised his underlings as they were rifling through drawers, combing cabinets and closets, and bundling up the papers near the body. It was a scene that reminded me of the night Bucholz and his henchmen came to the apartment in Vienna. As I tried to erase that vision from my mind, I glanced over to the study area and noticed the broken glass again. The shards lay near two vacant wooden frames.

One, document-size, may have hung from a hook behind the desk next to a similar frame that displayed a certificate of commendation for Helen's war work. The second broken frame on the floor was a gold metal tabletop model that must have held a photograph. Perhaps Helen had been working at the desk and, feeling ill, had knocked it off. But could she have lurched enough to lop the hanging frame off the wall? While I was trying to figure out how this might have happened, Tarrant turned his attention back to me.

"So, Mrs. Kovner, I hear that you've been threatened both here and in New York and warned not to continue this search. Now, you've discovered a dead body. Do you think there's any connection?"

How should I know? You're the policeman, I thought.

"I certainly hope not, Inspector," I said.

"You mentioned a woman who let you into the building. Can you describe her?"

"Taller than me, blonde hair, khaki mackintosh, matching rain hat pulled over her face on a slant, carrying a worn brown briefcase. Do you remember Marlene Dietrich in that film, *Witness for the Prosecution?*"

"I am not much for the cinema, ma'am," he said. "Your description is useful, though there are probably ten thousand women in London today that match it. But thank you. Do you have a telephone number at that flat? Once I get it, you can be on your way. However, I'd ask you to stay in London at least until I contact you again—only a day or two, I imagine. Right, now go out and Richardson here," nodding to one of the constables, "will drive you."

While supplying my number and mumbling assurances that I would remain in town, I noticed that the rain had stopped. Sunshine was creeping out.

"You know, Inspector, thank you, but as the rain has stopped, I'd really rather walk, if it's all the same to you. I fancy some fresh air."

"As you wish. Thank you for your time, Mrs. Kovner."

Fresh air was welcome. Not that the walk could in any way clear my head of the onslaught of overlapping sensations and questions.

Was it mere coincidence that Helen Wolf died just before I arrived to see her? Or was her death related? Was she murdered? Was I a suspect? This was not a film, but real life. What was happening? Maybe Helen was not well and just died. The wig. Perhaps she had cancer and suddenly just expired.

As I turned onto my block, I saw a skinny man with thick black-rimmed glasses wearing a dirty mackintosh. He was leaning against a car parked in front of my flat. His thin sallow face made him look ill, as if the cigarette he was smoking was sapping out his insides. As I approached, he tossed the butt into a puddle below the curb and placed himself smack in front of me on the pavement. I started, my heartbeat quickened, and I clutched my bag with both hands.

"Mrs. Kovner, no 'arm, promise." Although his voice was gruff, he grinned, revealing a mouthful of dilapidated amber-colored teeth. Straight out of the *Lavender Hill Mob* but with an accent bearing the unlikely mix of Cockney English and Israeli Hebrew.

Not persuaded by his assurance, I answered with a wary "Who are you?"

"Sam 'ere. I'm friends with Simon Rieger. Did the police question you? At 'elen Wolf's flat?"

"Yes."

"Are they thinking she's murdered?"

"Why would they think that? What do you know? Did you murder her? Who are you? Are you the person threatening me?"

My hand gripped the key to the flat inside my bag, and I glanced up and down the quiet street that, in the middle of the afternoon, lacked anyone close enough to help me.

Sensing my continuing fear, he said, "No, no. Look, it's not my intention to 'urt you. I'm a friend of Simon's, which makes me a friend of yours. I can't tell you how I know what I know, except to say that in my work I had reason to observe Miss Wolf's building before you arrived. There's the possibility she was murdered."

This speculation made me so short of breath that I couldn't even respond to it. So, I focused on something else.

"Why would you have the building—and me—under surveillance? Did Simon put you up to this?"

"I can't tell you any more, just Simon Rieger is concerned about your safety, is all. You must be careful, Mrs. Kovner. These people, they're dangerous."

"What people? The people who are sending me threatening messages? There was a blonde woman who let me into the building. Did she visit Helen Wolf? You must have seen her."

"Yes, I did, but who she is or if she had anything to do with this—can't say. If I wore your shoes, I'd pay attention to the threats. If they say to lay off your search, they know why. I've got to go now, but I'll be watching out for you."

And then he turned and walked away, toward Pont Street.

Chapter 13

I LET MYSELF into the flat and collapsed on the sofa. It was only two-thirty in the afternoon, but the events of the past two hours had enervated and confused me.

Was Helen Wolf murdered? If so, did it have anything to do with what she would tell me? Who was Sam? Was Simon having me followed? Did the threats I received have anything to do with what had happened to Helen?

It didn't take long before I got the answer to that. As I stood up to go into the kitchen to find something to eat, the phone rang. The same female voice delivered the message:

"You saw that woman on the floor. You could die, too. Forget your search. Go home."

It had to be that blonde woman who let me into Helen's building. Only she would know for sure that I had seen the body on the floor.

If I were the type, I would have fainted. Instead, I merely banged down the receiver and sank back onto the sofa. I knew I should call the authorities, so I rifled through my bag to find Cooks's phone number, judging her to be a more sympathetic contact than Tarrant. Before I could make the call, the phone rang again. It was Simon.

"Lily? I just talked to Sam, who told me that Helen Wolf died. Are you all right?"

"Well, between finding Helen dead and just getting a phone call which threatened me with the same fate, I would say I'm a little shaky. Who is Sam, Simon? What does he do, and how do you know him?"

"He's a friend who's looking out for you, believe me. I can't tell you more, not yet, but just know he's on your side. Though are you sure you shouldn't heed the advice and forget Afikomen?"

I demurred before responding. "If you have a friend watching me, I should be okay, right? With Helen's death, I've got even more reason to pursue this. I really didn't know her but I feel terrible about it, especially if it has anything to do with me. I think Helen would have been helpful. In fact, I. . . . "

I was going to tell him about the snapshot I'd found and swiped but thought better of it. Like Helen, I decided to be prudent about phone conversations.

"What?"

"Nothing. Look, Simon, I appreciate your call and concern. And, if Sam's truly a good guy, I appreciate him, too, although he's not the most comforting type. I need to get off now to call my police contacts here. The inspector investigating Helen's death wants me to stick around in London; I could be a suspect. But I've got to get out of here and on to Israel soon."

"Do what you have to do, but, please, Lily, take care of yourself, and be careful. I mean it. I'm very, very worried about all this," he said before ringing off.

Well, that was nice, I thought. But this was no time to linger over romance. I rang Sarah Cooks's private number.

"Yes, Mrs. Kovner," she said. "How are you doing? I spoke to Inspector Tarrant a short while ago, and he said you went off on foot back to your flat. I probably would have insisted on driving you, but . . . "

"I needed the fresh air," I cut in. "However, when I returned, I had another threatening phone call, a truly menacing one this time. The caller mentioned Helen Wolf and inferred that she'd indeed been murdered."

There was a slight pause before she said, "Really?"

To be the bearer of such news to Scotland Yard was a role I did not relish. Especially since I'd found the body.

Cooks asked, "What precisely did the caller say?"

"She—the same woman, I think—said, 'you saw that woman on the floor. You could die, too. Forget your search. Go home.'"

"She didn't actually say Helen Wolf was murdered," Cooks said.

"But don't you think that it tells you that, if she was murdered, I didn't do it? Can't you get Tarrant to let me leave London before the postmortem report comes in?"

"Well, Mrs. Kovner, we have only your say-so on this. You can't prove that you're receiving these phone threats—it's not like the anonymous letter in New York. There's no physical evidence. Plus, you were right there on the scene when Ms. Wolf was found dead. We have our procedures, you know."

Now I really despaired. I hadn't thought of that. "But I'm Elizabeth Aarons's mother. Doesn't that count for something?"

"Well," she started, before I changed my tack and spoke again, calmer and less emotional.

"In addition, Chief Inspector Cooks," I said, "I told Inspector Tarrant about the woman who let me into Helen Wolf's building. Helen's door was open. Someone must have left her flat in a hurry just before I arrived. Someone she'd let in, perhaps thinking it was me."

"But why are you so eager to leave London?"

"I have reason to believe that the Seder plate is in Israel. I only came to London first because of Helen Wolf and her research."

Again, I neglected to mention the photograph I picked up at Helen's. With Cooks this meant that I risked concealing evidence in solving Helen's murder, if it really was murder. However, that snapshot was the only evidence I had linking Bucholz to Rotan, a connection I was convinced would be key to Afikomen, and I was loathe to relinquish it. I'd also not said anything about my encounter with Sam. Cooks was the police, and maybe I should have been more forthcoming.

"I will see what I can do and ring you back later," she said crisply.

Five minutes later, after finally biting into a turkey sandwich I'd fixed, I heard from my daughter. Talk about emotional—Elizabeth was nearly screaming.

"Mother, I just talked to Sarah. Why didn't you call me?"

"There's been no time, honey," I said. "I've only been back for a short time, and. . . ."

"Sarah said you found Helen Wolf dead and you had another threatening phone call. This is nuts, Mother. Is Afikomen worth it?"

"You're the last person I'd expect to try to talk me out of it," I said. "You run all over Greater London tracking down unsavory characters to get a scoop."

"But now you're a target yourself. It's a whole different ballgame."

"Yes, but there's a mission in Afikomen. Finding it would generate an element of retribution for the crimes committed against our family."

"It wouldn't bring anyone back," Elizabeth said.

"Of course not. But, besides the pictures, mementoes, and notes in that album your grandmother gave me, it would be one more thing left from that whole life from before."

"I understand. What are you going to do now?"

I thought a minute, staring past my half-eaten sandwich to the recently modernized flat kitchen and fell back on a standard form of distraction when I knew I wouldn't be able to concentrate on anything else.

"Why don't you and Jonathan come over and I'll make dinner? I miss being able to cook for my kids. It'll do me good to get out to market and keep me busy."

"And a treat for us to get a good home-cooked meal. I'm afraid I didn't inherit your kitchen skills."

"Nonsense. If you can read, you can cook. You two are just never home. Come over when you can—six-thirty, seven."

Armed with a list and cloth shopping bags and feeling very local again, I headed out the door with renewed vigor. The sunshine and blue sky had left only a few puddles as vestiges of the morning's downpour. As I made my way toward Sloane Street, I caught a glimpse of Sam loitering with a news-paper. How cloak and dagger.

I wanted to trust Simon and anyone he would send to help me but couldn't understand why it had to be so secretive. I went about my errands sensing someone watching me the whole time. By the time I returned to the flat and began to make dinner, I had talked myself into a sense of security from the protective surveillance I thought I was getting. In truth, I didn't see Sam again.

When I got back into the flat, the phone was ringing. This time it was not threats, but Marty Zuckert, my editor at the *Smithsonian Magazine* calling from Washington. I'd left him a quick message that the story had taken an unusual twist and I was leaving for London and Israel to pursue it.

He was screaming when I answered. "Lily, what the hell are you doing in London? I said we'd pay some expenses, but I don't have the budget for a jaunt around the world."

I could visualize Marty holding the receiver with one hand and running the other through his leonine silver mane. A veteran of the heyday era of *Time* and *Life*, he considered his position at the slower paced monthly to be a kick upstairs for a has-been.

"Cool it, Marty," I said. "I'm on my own nickel here. The story has evolved into a more personal angle, anyway."

"What do you mean 'more personal'?"

"I went to an auction last Sunday and saw my family's antique Seder plate that was stolen by the Nazis. I came here to meet a woman helping people find looted art, but she was dead when I got to her flat. Too much to explain right now, but it'll be worth it to you, I promise, once I track down the owner of the Judaica house in Israel that sponsored the auction."

"Israel? You're going to Israel, too? Lily, this is supposed to be just a pretty piece about the Judaica market, the collectors, what's hot, what's coming into circulation from the former Soviet Union and Eastern Europe. Not a damn spy story. You know, I only called you for this because of old times and I figured you might want some work to keep you busy."

That frosted me. Considering everything else that had happened that day, I felt like really letting him have it. But I needed to keep the conversation cordial.

"Listen, Marty, you'll have to trust me. This should end up a great story. If you're so worried about the budget, you should get off the long-distance phone now. I'll be in touch. Bye."

At seven o'clock the kids arrived and inhaled with anticipation the rosemary scent of a lamb leg roasting in the oven. When we sat down with drinks, I pulled the snapshot of Helen and her companions out of my bag and passed it to them.

"I took this from Helen Wolf's," I said. "It stuck out from a pile of papers near her body."

"That's Trinity Fountain at Cambridge," said Jonathan, an alumnus of the august university.

"Who are these people, Mother?"

"I think they're Helen Wolf with Rudolf Bucholz, the Nazi art looter, and Professor Rotan, the scholar at the auction last week. Many years ago, obviously, but I'll never forget Bucholz's face. And I'm pretty sure about Rotan, although he's bald now."

"Well, they'd be too late for Venn's," Jonathan said.

I had no idea what he was talking about. "What's Venn's?"

"An alumni register that was started by John Venn, the mathematician—you know, the Venn diagram . . ."

"Not really," Elizabeth and I said in unison and then laughed, math having not been the strongest subject for either of us.

"You two! Anyway, Venn and later his son compiled volumes of biographies of Cambridge alumni through centuries. The son lived well into this century, but the last volume only goes until 1900."

"This would have been the late 1930s," I said. "I'd already learned that the three of them went to Cambridge and I suspected that there might have been a connection, which must have been what Helen Wolf would have told me. There must be something else that she knew. Maybe she'd been threatened, too. That could be why she wouldn't discuss specifics on the phone."

Elizabeth said, "Jonathan, even though this Venn's doesn't cover past 1900, there must be some registry up at Cambridge. Were there yearbooks like we have in America?"

"Now, yes. Then, no, I don't think so. But I should be able to get some information. I'll call tomorrow, see what I can get. Write down the names for me, Mum."

Elizabeth beamed at her husband's offer, and we moved to the table to eat. As if by magic, the instant I put the platter of lamb, vegetables, and orzo on the table and we'd sat down, the phone rang.

It was Uncle in New York.

"What's going on, Lily? How was the meeting with that lady?"

Even if I'd wanted to, I could hardly hide the news from Uncle. "Her name was Helen Wolf. I went to her flat and found her dead, unfortunately," I said.

"What? Dead! What happened?"

"I'm not really sure. Could be murder or just natural causes. There was a wig and her head was bald, so maybe she'd had chemotherapy for cancer. There's an autopsy going on now."

"What did you say? Murder?"

"The police aren't sure. Plus," I hesitated but decided that he should know, "I've had some threats about Afikomen—an anonymous letter in New York and a couple of crank phone calls here, telling me to stop. The last call, after I came in from Helen's, said something about did I want to end up like her. I've reported these to the police, but, because I found her, I'm a bit of a suspect. They won't let me leave London for Israel."

"That's it. When you leave, you're coming straight back to New York," he yelled. "Forget about Israel and Afikomen and the Seder plate. What do you need it for? I told you it would be dangerous. You don't understand about that time, the people involved."

"Uncle," I said, "the war's been over for 45 years. And I'm going to Israel to try to meet Professor Rotan, at least, and Ben-Shuvah at Mosaica. If they're all such upstanding people, there should be a proper resolution of this. I'm not coming straight back to New York. No way. Besides, some guy that Simon knows is watching my back."

We hung up, so I could go back to dinner. I thought I had convinced him to calm down until my son, Jacob, called from San Francisco twenty minutes later.

"Uncle just got me paged out of a meeting. You're being threatened? Mom, are you okay? Are you nuts? Why go on with this?"

"I'm fine. Talk to your sister," I said, passing the phone to Elizabeth, who promptly got up and turned her back as she walked away. She thought I couldn't hear her.

"Jacob, she's fine. She seems to be playing out some kind of an emotional need with this. Mother's tough. She's not to be deterred by anything we say or do, so cool it."

Coming back to the table, she switched back to normal volume, "How are the twins? Amy? We can't wait to see you in New York for Passover."

When Elizabeth got off the phone, I mentioned that I hoped her friend, Sarah, could be helpful in getting me permission to leave.

"I can't ask for that favor, if that's what you mean, Mother," she said.

"No, I understand that. It's just that I'm going crazy here in limbo."

Jonathan said, "So, you stay here a few more days. You can go to theatre, have fancy tea somewhere with my mum. You're not confined to the flat."

I didn't want to insult him or his mother, my old friend Liesel, but I knew I couldn't muster the patience for theatre and tea just then.

"I know there are worse things than a few extra days in London. There's plenty to do, and it's wonderful being in the same city with the two of you.

However, this Afikomen—it's like the Seder itself. There's an order, a progression to it, despite the detours and bumps in the road. It's my mission right now. I sense that Israel is where it will all come out, one way or the other, and I need to get on with it."

"We get it, Mother, but you don't want to mess with Scotland Yard," said Elizabeth.

"I know, I know. I'm just so edgy and frustrated. I had put a lot of faith in the meeting with Helen Wolf. Now that's a dead end—literally."

"Ooh," said Jonathan, "bad pun. Let's talk about something else. Elizabeth tells me there's a new man in your life."

I wasn't sure that this was the alternative topic I would have chosen at that moment, but, as we ate, I regaled them with the story of Simon's adventures in the United States Army and later in the Israeli War of Independence.

"Why was he at the same Judaica auction you went to?" Elizabeth asked.

"He collects rare Sephardic manuscripts. I'd use him as a source for my magazine piece, although, with my own Afikomen in progress, I don't know how my assignment will turn out."

An hour later they had to leave. "Get some rest, Mother," Elizabeth said, kissing me goodbye. "We'll talk to you tomorrow."

The next morning, when I returned from my swim, Sarah Cooks called.

"Good morning, Mrs. Kovner," she said crisply. "I hadn't wanted to promise yesterday, but we were able to get the postmortem exam done last night, and the result is good news—for you.

"Turns out that your theory about Helen Wolf being a cancer patient holds up. She was in treatment and, in fact, wore one of those morphine pumps you can use to administer medication oneself as needed. Apparently, the pump malfunctioned, as the cause of death was an overdose of morphine that stopped the heart."

"So, she wasn't murdered? The threatening caller said—no, actually she didn't say Helen was murdered. She said I wouldn't want to end up dead like Helen." Though still confused, I rejoiced at the semantic difference.

"Not that we can tell," said Cooks. "This means, Mrs. Kovner, that you are free to leave London whenever you wish."

"Thank you for all that you've done," I said.

"Travel safely, and stay safe."

The phone call relieved me, but I still questioned how Helen Wolf could have sounded so chipper two hours before I found her, if she was in such terrible pain. As much as I wanted to believe that her death was accidental, I couldn't help wondering if someone had escalated the morphine dose. I'm no doctor but I'd never heard of those pumps malfunctioning. And what about that blonde woman who was leaving the building as I went in?

In ten minutes I'd reserved a flight to Tel Aviv for the next morning. That gave me time for one last dinner with the kids. When Jonathan arrived at the table in an Indian restaurant where Elizabeth and I had already been seated, he withdrew a small piece of paper from his jacket pocket and handed it to me.

There were eight names: Anthony Ballentine, Rudolf Bucholz, Victor Henderson, Margaret Lewellyn, Stefan Rothenberg, Charles Smythe-Perkins, William Thomas, and Helen Wolf.

"What's this?"

"The Cambridge art graduates of 1937," he said. "Nothing like an Eliezer Ben-Shuvah, that's for sure."

"That's probably a modern Israeli name," I said, "adapted from something else, like Golda Meir from Meyerson. Rotan, too, but maybe Stefan Rothenberg—S. R.—that could be Rotan. Thank you, Jonathan, this will be very useful."

PART V

Israel, 1990

Chapter 14

Entering israel is never easy. The thrill of first sighting as the plane descends over the Tel Aviv shore evaporates as you embark at Ben-Gurion to face not only the universal passport control and customs procedures but also vigorous questioning about why you've come, how long you plan to stay, whom you know in Israel, how you know them, where they live.

Normally I am patient and sanguine about the security requisites; this time I yearned to break free quickly. However, my recent encounter with the British authorities stifled any inclination I might have harbored to even think of complaining. Not that the line was long. The year-long intifada had imploded tourism.

Cleared after a record-breaking brief fifteen minutes, I hailed a taxi and gave the driver Mosaica's address. His grin and courteous service signaled that I'd negotiated, in my broken Hebrew and his similar English, to vastly overpay for him to wait for me there and then drive me to my flat in Jerusalem.

The white stucco Bauhaus-style building, well restored compared to many of its counterparts in the city, sparkled in the afternoon sunshine. Sign age was subtle, but a small notice on the front door validated Shira Reznik's information that the auction house was closed for the week. Seeing lights on inside, I banged on the door anyway. Eventually, a pretty Asian woman about forty appeared, unlocked it, and stepped outside.

"Closed, madam, so sorry, " she said. "Have major auction next week. Whole staff prepares for it."

"Yes, I know that, but I'm here because of last week's auction in New York. There was a Seder plate that was stolen from my family by the Nazis. It came on the block, and was taken away after I protested. Shira Reznik in your New York office told me it was brought back to Israel."

The woman's dark eyes widened, and she appeared startled and upset. Recovering, she said, "Surely, there's misunderstanding. But nothing to be done right now. Mr. Ben-Shuvah, owner of Mosaica, out of the country."

"May I ask who you are and what your position here is?"

"I am called Ruth Sofer. I am chief curator, specialist in Judaica. And you, madame?"

"Lily Kovner, nice to meet you, Ruth," I said, warming.

Out of a gap in the neckline of her aqua cotton blouse slipped a gold chain holding a locket inlaid with a spray of branches and a rose set with a miniscule diamond chip. Instinctively, I reached under my turtleneck to pull out my own chain that dangled a locket with a lily-of-the-valley spray and diamond-centered flower. My grandmother gave it to me for my eighth birthday, the last one in Vienna.

Ruth again looked shocked, but pleased. "Amazing," she said, "how much our lockets alike. My father's mother gave him this before he left Europe to go to Shanghai. I have picture of his parents, my grandparents, inside."

She opened her locket to reveal the same photograph that I had in mine. Opening it to show her, I said, "Was your father Erich Heilbrun?"

"Yes."

"He was my uncle."

"*Wo ba,*" she said. "My father. Your mother—Elisabeth?"

I nodded. We stood and stared at each other for a moment before embracing in tears. This woman, this Chinese woman, was my first cousin. Her father and my mother—twin brother and sister. Too much of a coincidence to comprehend.

"Come inside," she said. "We talk."

Which overwhelmed me more? Being inside Mosaica or finding Uncle Erich's daughter, Ruth? My shock must have showed, because as soon as Ruth led me through the lobby into her office and I dived onto the nearest chair, she poured me a cup of jasmine tea from a porcelain pot on her desk.

"Thank you," I said. "I could probably use something stronger, but this will work for now."

She laughed. "There's brandy or sherry somewhere."

I shook my head. "Really, the tea's perfect."

Ruth poured herself a cup. "So much to talk about—where to start. My father and Elisabeth, they were twins, right?"

"Yes," I said. "And kindred spirits. I remember when he left for Shanghai. He'd wanted to come here to Palestine, but our grandmother had a stroke, and he felt guilty about leaving. Finally, when Shanghai was the only place left to go, he just said good-bye one day and left the next. He was really the first one in the family who saw the futility of staying in Austria. My parents and grandparents—*our* grandparents—they all stayed and were murdered by the Nazis. My mother sent me off to London, to our Aunt Lottie's."

By now tears were streaming down Ruth's face. "I always knew I'd find someone from his family," she said.

"What happened to your father? Aunt Lottie tried to trace him after the war. Most of the Jews who went to China left by 1949."

"He met my mother. They married in 1947. She was pregnant with me when the Communists came. Complications—she couldn't travel, they stayed. My *ba* he died when I was twelve."

She reached into her desk drawer and pulled out a snapshot of a Chinese woman who looked just like Ruth with her arm around a thin and haggard-looking old man holding the hand of a cupie doll child with a bow in her hair. I recognized my uncle's face under the thatch of white hair. Underneath them was written Suzhou Gardens, 1954. Uncle Erich would have been fifty years old. He looked eighty.

"China not good for his health," Ruth said. "Stomach problems, emphysema, often pneumonia. A weakened immune system, we say today. Eventually, he died. Heart attack. 1960. Lucky he missed the Cultural Revolution."

"And you and your mother?"

"My mother came from family of professors. She taught literature—classic Chinese novels, poetry. Somehow, she kept position at Beida—Peking University—many years under Communists, until 1968. Then they sent her for reeducation in the countryside. She never made it back to Beijing. I stayed in Shanghai with friends."

I put my hand on Ruth's. We had more than our lineage in common.

"How did you get to Israel?" I really wanted to ask why.

"Long story . . ."

"Aren't they all?"

"I'd been sent to Russia—Leningrad—to study. Eighteen years old then. Through Russian students I met Jewish *refusniks*. They had applied to leave the Soviet Union and were kicked out of university. I went to their houses and saw old Jewish books and religious things their families kept hidden or new ones American Jews smuggled in. I was like them. I was part-Jewish but had no idea what being Jewish meant. Only I longed to know more about my father's background. I met lawyer from Boston. Later he helped me immigrate to the States. I did graduate work in art history at Harvard and met my husband, Boaz. He was at MIT getting doctorate in computer science. He's on faculty at Weizmann Institute."

"Ruth and Boaz—the Book of Ruth."

"My mother-in-law's named Naomi. So why I picked name Ruth when I converted."

"Do you have children?"

"Twins," she said. "More twins, Eli and Talia. Eli named for my father, Erich, and your mother, Elisabeth. They're ten years old. You have children?"

"My children, Elizabeth and Jacob, named for my parents, are grown. Jacob also has twins, Joshua and Gabriella, three years old. Gabby is named for our grandmother, Gertrude."

"Do we have more family?"

"The London branch—Aunt Lottie Koopman, Charlotte, and her two sons, Julian and Daniel, who have children and grandchildren. Aunt Lottie lives here in Israel in the winter, and the brothers commute; they're in the diamond business. I'm planning to see her on Shabbat. Why don't you and your family come, too? Lunch at my flat in Jerusalem."

"Heilbrun family reunion—something I have dreamed about. Never thought possible!"

Ruth's enthusiasm and our immersion in family history almost made me forget why I was there. Did the Seder plate even matter any more? If Afikomen turned out to unearth only this newfound family, wouldn't it be *dayenu*—enough?

She read my silence. "Tell me what happened in New York. Why you came here."

After I'd finished a quick summary of the auction, my encounter with Reznik, and the results of the search warrant, she looked puzzled.

"I wonder that I haven't heard about this," she said. "Shaul Rotan came in when he returned. Never mentioned a word. Neither did Yael."

"Who's Yael?"

"Yael Ben-Shuvah, Eliezer's daughter. She works here. She's really his right-hand woman, I guess you say in the States. I'll introduce you before you leave. I didn't see that Seder plate come back to the gallery. I thought probably it was sold at the auction. I don't handle the business end. Research, writing, editing the catalogues—that's my job."

"If you handle research, wouldn't you be responsible for provenance documentation?"

"Not always. I study origins of the pieces, artisans who created them, their place, context, where they came from and when, how they relate to Jewish culture and history from the time. Provenance, at least at Mosaica, handled as an inventory business issue—by Eliezer and Yael."

"I'm sure that you're aware that the Nazis looted prodigiously and that much of the art work they stole never found its way back to its original owners?"

"Of course, but, if this operation were selling it, I'd not work here. And I can't imagine Shaul Rotan would have anything to do with it either. He's so eminent in his field. When I came to Israel, I studied under him. We're very close. I can call him to arrange meeting for you with him. What's today? Wednesday. Maybe tomorrow? Okay? He loves to have lunch at King David Hotel. You'll be in Jerusalem, right?"

"Yes, I have a flat of my own. I'd be so grateful if you could arrange an appointment with Professor Rotan. Here's a card with my Jerusalem phone number."

As we walked through the corridor between Ruth's office and the lobby, we passed a dark-haired young woman bent over a filing drawer who turned her head toward us. Her angular nose and chin looked familiar, but like those of any number of people.

"Yael, this my cousin, Lily," said Ruth.

"Shalom," Yael said curtly.

When we reached the door, Ruth walked me outside. My driver leaned against the car door smoking. My cousin and I hugged and I thanked her again for her offer to call Rotan.

"But I'd appreciate it if you don't mention this to anyone else, like Yael, for instance."

"I understand," she said. "I speak with you later."

By the time the driver and I had wound our way up to Jerusalem and

I'd handed him the agreed-upon sum in front of my building, it was nearly six o'clock. My flat is a second floor walk-up in a Mandate-era building, its exterior the pale limestone known as Jerusalem stone, now weathered and bleached to a dirty gold.

I'd bought it in the 1950s after receiving reparations from West Germany to compensate for the deaths of my parents. As if 20,000 deutsche marks, the equivalent then of less than $5,000, could compensate for the lives of two lively people murdered simply because they were Jews. Still, it was the closest thing I had to an inheritance, and a sum that went a lot further as a down payment then in the leafy Rehavia section, favored by settlers from Europe for decades. Spending my mother's blood money on a home in Jerusalem would have pleased her.

I hadn't been back in six months. The musty place needed airing out. With the windows and balcony door flung wide open, soon the breeze and the fragrance of rose bushes wafted in. After unpacking, I grabbed the rusting pull-cart from its spot next to the front door to take off for the Mahane Yehuda indoor-outdoor market a half-mile away. Though a frequent target of suicide bombers, the bustling market always overflows with irresistible displays of Israel's edible bounty, as well as Jerusalem's eclectic consumers.

Winding through the lanes of shops and vendors lining the aisles propelled me through sights and smells that both whetted my appetite and reoriented me to Jerusalem life. Whole fish flopped around tanks in front of their filleted brethren on ice. Plump yellow birds, destined for Shabbat chicken soup, stretched raw next to bloody slabs of beef and lamb. A cheese purveyor offered a sample of salty feta after I had committed to buy a hand-dipped glop of chèvre and a slab of Camembert. Mounds of fruit not yet in season in New York or London—ripe melons, plump peaches, scarlet raspberries—beckoned. Vats of cured olives and pickles redolent with garlic sat next to cases of prepared eggplant, beet, and pepper salads. The yeasty perfume of baking bread overpowered honeyed platters of baklava.

Mentally composing a menu while picking up staples such as yogurt and coffee, I suddenly sensed that I was being followed. Down one aisle, every time I stopped at a food display, my peripheral vision revealed a short, stocky man of about fifty, with thick, wavy black hair and olive skin. He was dressed in jeans and a black leather jacket. Something about his face was familiar, but I couldn't place it. Catching me looking at him, he would stop in his tracks and quickly address himself to the nearest products, buying nothing and sneaking furtive glances my way.

Wondering whether to try to lose him, never mind how, I sidled toward a butcher shop, where at least four women stood lined up ahead of me. This gave me a chance to observe my observer, now waylaid in front of a tank of fish fluttering for dear life. The crowd emboldened me, and I sauntered over to him.

"Excuse me, do I know you?" I said in Hebrew.

He replied in English. "You are Mrs. Kovner, correct?"

"Yes," continuing in English myself, "but who are you, and how do you know who I am?"

"I am Avi, a friend of Simon Rieger," he said. "You must be careful, Mrs. Kovner, you could be in danger."

"I've heard that before," I said, "and also that a woman in London was murdered, when she wasn't. Why should I trust you?"

"I am trying to protect you, madam," Avi pleaded. "And Helen Wolf *was*, in fact, murdered."

"The coroners in London declared her death the result of natural causes."

"They are mistaken. She was murdered. Believe me, I know. We have sources."

"Who are 'we'?"

"That, Mrs. Kovner, I do not have the authority to reveal. But you must trust that, on the instruction of Simon Rieger, we are trying to protect you."

"Look, Avi, I'm not trying to be difficult. In fact, I've wondered myself about the autopsy report on Helen Wolf. I don't know who Simon's contacts are. Maybe you're Mossad or from some other official agency. If you're looking out for me, I should be grateful, and I am. But I plan on taking care of myself."

"Take my card, Mrs. Kovner. You can call me at any time."

I tucked the card in my bag, turned away, and darted into the herring shop on my right, glancing back to see Avi walk in the opposite direction, apparently speaking into the receiver at his ear, one of those new cell phones that were omnipresent in Israel. The sight of the phone amused me and made me proud of the cutting-edge country, but my conversation with Avi was exasperating. I tried to focus on the smelly cured fish, evaluating the bits of samples proffered by the counter man, and selecting my favorite variety, slathered in sour cream.

But I couldn't ignore what Avi had said. If Helen really was murdered, why wouldn't the autopsy report convey that? How would this Avi, this friend of Simon, know? Simon Rieger, jeweler, playboy bon vivant, and what? Ring leader of international agents? Tracking my every movement. Disputing Scotland Yard.

Finally, I'd lost Avi among stalls overflowing with more varieties of eggplant, kohlrabi, tomatoes, and oranges than one could imagine. Free of him lurking behind me, I could concentrate on what to buy and cook and on the amusing sight of a bewigged, long-skirted woman fussily pressing, sniffing, and rejecting one cucumber after another.

By the time I got home, I'd convinced myself that tomorrow's lunch with Rotan would lead me straight to the Seder plate, making Saturday's family celebration a double reunion. Surely, the ringing phone that greeted me would confirm this plan. It was Ruth.

"Sorry, Lily, but Shaul can't meet until Sunday," she said. "He has brother in the north to visit tomorrow—brother's an invalid. Shaul takes care of him in wonderful place near Karmiel. And he picks up his grandchildren in Haifa for Shabbat on the way home, so Friday's no good either. The first opportunity Sunday, noon at the King David. I'll come, too."

Deflated, I almost started to cry. I wondered if Rotan was evading me. "Did you mention my name?"

"No, I only told him that I want him to meet cousin from the States. I know you're disappointed," Ruth said, "but nothing I can do about it. But by then Eliezer will return, too, so you can get this all straightened out."

"Yes, I suppose so. Anyway, I'll see you on Shabbat. Thank you, Ruth."

It was crushing to realize that, after my permission to leave London materialized earlier than expected, Afikomen was now stalled in Israel. To compound my frustration, the phone rang again, with the now familiar raspy woman's voice welcoming me to Jerusalem.

"So, Mrs. Kovner, you haven't learned. Go home. Israel is not safe for you."

I fumbled in my bag for Avi's card and read it—Avi Ben-Ze'ev and a phone number. No affiliation. Instead of calling, I double-locked my door and went to bed.

Chapter 15

THE NEXT MORNING I launched my day in the Byzantine-tiled pool at the Jerusalem YMCA, the phallic landmark that can be seen from all over the city. Leaving the Y refreshed but still consumed by the postponement of my meeting with Rotan, I glanced longingly at another landmark, the historic King David Hotel, across the street. Turning onto my block from Ramban Street, I saw a man leaning against a car in front of my building. Not another one, I thought.

Closer, I realized it was Simon Rieger himself in khaki pants and a black sport shirt embossed with the Polo pony, the type of logo apparel Arthur and I disdained. Knowing the circles Simon ran in, I figured Ralph Lauren was a personal friend.

The instant Simon noticed me approaching he tossed a cigarette onto the pavement and ground the butt with his foot.

"Caught in the act," he said, holding out his arms to greet me with a kiss redolent of tobacco.

On the one hand, I was surprised and delighted to see him and let myself be enveloped. On the other, it bothered me that he might think I couldn't handle this on my own, and was just a woman in need of protection.

"I hope you're happy to see me but I'm not sure," he said after I'd wriggled out of his embrace.

"I am, Simon. But I don't like to be patronized."

"What are you talking about 'patronized'? Oh, you think I'm just here because you're some poor helpless little lady?"

"Let's go inside," I said.

"Nice flat," he said when I'd opened my door. "Very Jerusalem."

"What's that supposed to mean?"

"The neighborhood, the style of the building, your Danish modern furniture, the balcony overlooking the small garden, the books—it has the feel of the city. Meditative, intellectual. That's all. Nothing derogatory. I love Jerusalem."

"Well, it's not exactly Central Park South, or West, but it's an oasis. For me a place in Israel had to be in Jerusalem, and Rehavia is the most European part, where my mother would have wanted to be. A place on the beach would be like a beach anywhere."

Remembering that he owned a villa on the sea, I instantly reddened.

"Oops, sorry," I said. "Not that there's anything wrong with the beach. I love water."

"Herzlia is very convenient for me when I need to work at my Tel Aviv office. I know you think I'm the highest flyer in New York, but I don't have a country place in the States or a house in Palm Beach. I despise the Hamptons, which must surprise you. But the sea in Israel provides me great pleasure with a reasonable commute. Look at you with a place here, a place in London, and your apartment in New York. That's pretty impressive."

"I'm glad I can impress the great Simon Rieger."

"Okay, can we dispense with the sarcasm now? It may be warm and sunny outside, but it's damn chilly in here."

"Who the hell are these guys, Sam and Avi, who've been following me around saying they're your friends but they can't tell me who they work for? And you haven't told me either."

Almost whispering, he said, "They're Mossad."

I burst out laughing.

"Right, and I'm Mata Hari! How in God's name have you managed to sic a pack of Mossad agents after me?"

"They're friends, okay? I've been concerned about your safety. Can we drop it at that?"

I nodded, let out a big sigh, and gave him a hug.

"That's better," he said. "Now, I know that you're not meeting with Rotan until Sunday and your family is coming over on Shabbat . . ."

"Is my phone bugged?"

"I'd call it 'monitored.' As I was saying, since you have time on your hands, maybe we can spend some together."

"When did you get to Israel?"

"Tuesday. I needed to see my people here and I thought I'd surprise you. I'd hoped you'd be happy to see me."

"I am, Simon. Sorry, I guess I'm a trifle edgy—to say the least."

"An understatement, but understandable. That's why I want you to know that you can rely on the people watching you. Now, let's get you out for some fun. The place is lovely, but I don't want you cooped up brooding about the Seder plate, Afikomen, and bad guys for the next three days. I have a plan."

"Okay," I said, making an effort to sound warmer, because, in truth, I was thrilled to see him.

"If you're willing to slum and spend a little time by the sea, I thought we'd drive over to Haifa . . . "

"Haifa! That far?"

"Lily, this is Israel, remember? Where we can drive the whole country in a day. It's only ten o'clock. If we leave now, we'll get there for lunch. Maybe we can take a walk in the gardens at the Baha'i Temple. Then drive down to my place, relax on the beach or at the pool, have dinner outside at my favorite spot overlooking the water. Stay over. Come back tomorrow. How does that sound?"

It sounded divine. Seeing Simon again, despite the rocky start, reignited the tinge of desire I'd experienced when we went out in New York the week before.

"Stay over?"

"Well," he said, "there's no need to drive back in the dark. Just so you know, Lily, I have three bedrooms in the house."

"We'll work it out, I'm sure. Just so I'm back in time tomorrow night to prepare for my Shabbat lunch."

"I guarantee it."

You see a lot of Mercedes in Israel, thanks to the country's strong business relationship with Germany dating back to the reparations era, but the small red convertible parked outside was an anomaly. Figures, I thought, until Simon walked past the Mercedes and opened the door on the passenger side of a dark green Volvo sedan at least ten years old.

"This is your car? Not the red one?"

"Who'd have a car like that in Israel? I hope you're not disappointed," he said.

"Not at all."

We drove out of Jerusalem and angled northeast toward Haifa, maneuvering around spots where the West Bank juts east. Simon obviously knew the route well, pointing out Druze villages and biblical sites along the way. There was no direct highway yet from Jerusalem to Haifa, so we picked up the coastal road into Haifa and climbed up its Mount Carmel about one o'clock.

As predicted, we arrived in time for lunch. We parked the car and strolled hand in hand around the promenade, with its San Francisco–like vista of the Mediterranean, until we reached our lunch spot.

"This is the best falafel stand in Israel," he announced in the midst of an effusive handshake with the vendor. "Lily, meet Mutty."

In short order Mutty handed each of us a large pita stuffed with Israel's signature fast food and pointed to his smorgasbord of pickled vegetables and sauces to put on top. Balancing our drippy sandwiches and canned drinks, Simon and I made our way to a nearby bench.

"This was a great idea," I said. I bit off some falafel and dribbled tahina down my chin, barely arresting the stream before it dripped onto my jeans.

"Nice catch," said Simon. "Can you handle Afikomen failing as deftly as that? What if you never find the Seder plate?"

"Not a chance. Since I saw the Seder plate that day at the auction, I've simply decided that I'm going to get it back."

"It's one thing to be resolved," said Simon, "but another to lose sight of reality. The threats that you've received mean that there's good reason for you not to find it, or at least not to find out who has it."

"Or the threats could mean that I'm closing in on it," I said. "I must keep myself convinced that I can find it."

After lunch we descended to the terraced gardens of the Baha'i Temple. This gold-domed building is the world headquarters of that unity-based faith, yet another local player in the land of religions. The peacefulness of this cypress-lined spot blotted out even the suggestion of the sting of disappointment that failure could bring.

An hour and a half later, about four o'clock, we pulled off the road onto a residential lane that backed on the sea and soon turned into the driveway of an ivory stucco one-story villa. The landscaping was simple—indigenous ground cover and rocks placed precisely enough to produce a natural, though undoubtedly expensive, effect.

"Magnificent," I said, when Simon opened the front door to reveal the wall of windows that overlooked a swimming pool only steps away from the equally turquoise Mediterranean.

"Up for your second swim of the day, or don't you want to risk your hairdo?"

"My hair? It's designed for swimming. First, though, I'd love to see the rest of the house."

Though minimally furnished in a neutral palette of gray and beige, the décor offered a perfect backdrop for the Israeli paintings and sculpture that dotted the living and dining rooms. All very contemporary—including some a trifle bizarre to my taste. But the place could have been a gallery.

"I thought you collected rare Hebrew manuscripts hundreds of years old. Even the Reuven Rubins here look old school compared to some of these paintings, and he died, when, less than twenty years ago?"

"He died sometime in the seventies. The manuscripts I keep in the library in my New York apartment, which I'll show you when we get back. It's a wood-paneled sanctuary. But in this house I have only Israeli art, some very fresh and cheap. I love tripping over new talent."

Every room faced the sea, and skylights capped the interior hallways and bathrooms. Just as overpowering as the radiance had been when we arrived was the abrupt darkness after a single clap of thunder announced a downpour that began to pound down on the pool and terrace and splatter all those windows.

"So much for your swim," he said, while heaving the glass door shut. "Sorry."

He joined me on the sofa and put his arm around me. We turned to face each other and melded into an embrace and kiss.

I heard myself say, "There are other ways to spend a rainy afternoon," at which point Simon pulled away just enough to take my hand and lead me into the master bedroom.

Since the onslaught of my husband's illness, two years had passed since I'd made love. I'd briefly dated one other man for whom I had no desire. Did the passage of time without a man account for the physical awakening I'd experienced with Simon every time we were together? Somehow, I didn't think so. Our chemistry seemed to have a life of its own.

The depth of my arousal, on simmer from the beginning of our relationship, bubbled up as we fell onto the down-topped bed, its king size an anomaly in Israel then, even in the best hotels. Pressing our bodies together still fully clothed revealed that he was excited, too. While undressing each other, we lingered to kiss and fondle every newly exposed morsel of flesh from head to toe. Any shyness or discomfiture that my sexual hiatus might have engendered quickly evaporated. I readily surrendered to the pleasure of old sensations I was thrilled to welcome back. And I cared equally about ensuring that Simon would feel equally gratified.

His touch, magical for someone with two good arms, was miraculous for someone disabled. He could sense from my every sigh and movement where I was and where I was headed, bringing me to a tantalizing brink and then keeping me at bay before returning me to a place just before the moment the dam would burst. As we both knew that moment was close, he raised his head from between my legs, gently lifted mine from between his, and quickly repositioned himself to again lie facing me, placing two fingers and a thumb where his tongue had been.

"I want to watch you," he said, kissing my lips.

"What about you?" I gasped, bringing my own hand up to stroke him, even as the first waves of orgasm throbbed within me.

"Shh . . . after." He was smiling.

I reached a crescendo so intense and enduring that I had forgotten such ecstasy was possible, if I'd ever known it quite like this. As it subsided down to small pulses, I managed to boost myself up over Simon and glided his penis into me, contracting myself on it as rhythmically as my outer body moved up, down, and around, at times grazing his chest with my nipples or licking his neck. Just as his release neared, Simon pulled my head down to his lips and smothered my face with kisses. His thrusting surge was accompanied by breathless groans of pleasure.

For a few minutes afterward, we rested in that position, then he rolled us back to face each other, entwined inside and out as long as possible. Sweaty but beaming, we embraced and pressed close. It took a while before either of us could speak.

"I've wanted this since the first time we met," he said eventually.

At that moment, though I may have thought "I bet you say that to all the girls," I readily gave him the benefit of the doubt.

"Mmm, that was so good, Simon," was the most sparkling retort I could muster.

"Thank you," he said, smiling as he caressed my face with one hand and breasts with another. "You are a wonderful lover, and gorgeous," he said.

"For an old broad."

"For any age."

Who could argue with that? I nodded as, entangled, we lay back and fell asleep, the splash of raindrops on the windows no deterrent to a blissfully satisfied nap.

Awakening, I rolled over and faced a smiling Simon propped up on his right elbow, fixated on me.

"Hello," he greeted. "Ready for another go?"

I laughed. "Are you up for it?" I raised the covers, peering down, and announced, "Yes, you are."

Laughing, he opened his arms to me.

An hour later, after another short interlude of dozing, Simon leapt out of bed and bounded for the bathroom. "Another symptom of old age."

"Who's old today?"

After we'd showered together, he put on a white terry cloth robe, stepped out onto the terrace, and announced that the rain had stopped. He went into the kitchen and a few minutes later came back to the bedroom with two glasses of white wine.

"L'chaim," he said, as we clinked. "To a long life of lovemaking and love."

"I'll drink to that," I said.

"And to a successful hunt for Afikomen."

"I'm reluctant to admit this," I said, "but this afternoon almost made me forget about it. Not quite, but what a release of tension."

"I'm delighted to provide a therapeutic service. Now, for the next part of the treatment, Dr. Rieger prescribes dinner for his patient."

We got dressed and drove to a Provence-style restaurant that looked like a shack from the outside. A strapping teenaged boy checked for what might be in my bag. Inside, it was noisy and smoky, and all eight tables were taken. The chef-proprietor, Michel, a bearded man whose belly advertised his profession, greeted Simon with an enthusiastic bear hug and seated us at the lone separate table on a sandy stone patio no more than fifty feet from the sea. We both ordered the house specialty, bouillabaisse, authentically replete with non-kosher shellfish, bathed in garlicky, saffron-colored broth along with fish as fresh as the daily catch in Nice.

"I feel a tad guilty eating this in Israel," I said, while prying a mussel out of its shell. "But it is delicious."

Simon sipped his white burgundy, also French, and nodded. "Restaurant food in Israel has certainly matured, don't you think?"

"The whole country offers so much," I said. "Too bad that all its woes and now this intifada keep tourists away. Although this place is hopping. If only people who fear coming to Israel knew how safe it feels here with the security precautions—the soldiers patrolling the streets, private guards at restaurants. Even a little place like this."

"The security guard here—that's Michel's kid, Noam. Leaving for the Army next month," said Simon. "Even though this is off the beaten track and mainly patronized by locals, Michel takes no chances. He's got a Holocaust story, too."

I sighed. "Doesn't everyone?"

"He and his parents and two brothers were hidden in a convent near what had been their country home in Aix for two years. His older sister, passing as a gentile and on a mission for the Resistance back in Paris, was denounced to a gendarme by the father's former secretary. The Gestapo picked her up and shot her within a half-hour. The rest of the family survived, came here in about 1950, and pretty much lived happily ever after. Like you, except for the Seder plate."

"Even including the Seder plate," I said. "It could be worse, and Afikomen has led me to find my cousin. Not a bad result so far."

By the time we got back to Simon's villa, it was after ten o'clock. We sat on lounge chairs on his poolside terrace and watched and listened as the moonlit waves lapped up on the sand, adding rhythmic counterpoint to the density of the inky sky dotted with stars.

"The rain sure cleared the air. What a gorgeous night," Simon said. "And a wonderful day and evening with you, Lily."

He reached for my hand and kissed it.

"It's been great, Simon. Thank you for whisking me out of Jerusalem. Do you realize that no one knows where I am, not my kids, not Uncle, not my aunt, not my editor . . . ?"

"The Mossad knows," he said.

"Yes. Undoubtedly why another threatening note didn't crawl out of my clamshell. But, it's strange for me to be out of touch. It feels, I don't know . . . irresponsible."

"Listen, if you're feeling guilty, you're welcome to use the phone here to call anyone you want," he said.

"Thanks, but right now I find that I can live with this kind of guilt. A little irresponsibility could be good for me. I just don't want my family to think I fell prey to the perpetrators of the threats. But tomorrow will be soon enough."

Tomorrow burst forth, after a night's sleep induced by another round of lovemaking, with a flood of sunlight. We woke up after eight.

"I never sleep this late," I said.

"More guilt?"

I swatted him with a pillow. "Now who's stereotyping? I don't think I'm that uptight."

"Not here, you're not," he said, pulling me toward him.

Another half-hour passed before we got up. "I will go make some coffee," said Simon, pulling on his robe.

"You don't have to wait on me, you know."

"Why not? You get ready for your swim, if you want. By the way, you don't have to wear a suit here. It's completely private."

Swimming nude with goggles is not likely to become an Olympic uniform, but it did wonders for my strokes and made for an enthusiastic cheering section of one, who joined me in the pool briefly before producing a breakfast of omelets and fresh fruit that would easily sustain us until dinner.

"No Rumanian gvetch?" I said, when we sat down at the outdoor table.

"Not for breakfast. Tell me what you'd like to do today before we get back to Jerusalem. Go into Tel Aviv? Stay here? You name it, Lily."

"There is something I always try to do before Shabbat when I am in Israel. Go to Yad Vashem. I hope you don't mind."

"Didn't I say I'd take you anywhere you want to go?"

"And there's one more thing. I want to pick up some fresh fish for tomorrow."

"We can do that at a place near here, and my guy will pack it in a small ice chest to keep it cold until we get to your flat."

Yad Vashem is Israel's memorial to the six million, and it closed early on Fridays. We left Herzlia about eleven-thirty and pulled into its Jerusalem parking lot by one o'clock.

Until I became a widow, I'd never practiced the custom of visiting a cemetery, placing pebbles on a grave to symbolize remembrance or the rocklike endurance of a soul, depending on which rabbinic interpretation one embraces. Where would I go? My father died in Dachau and my mother in a pit in what's now the Republic of Belarus. To me Yad Vashem is the family memorial park.

When I go, I absorb every exhibit as if it's my first time. When I walk through the twinkling section of Yad Vashem called the Children's Memorial, where starry lights flash on photos of slain innocents, I think about the couple who donated it after losing their tiny son in Auschwitz but surviving themselves to prosper in California. I visualize my childhood face on that wall. What if I'd been slain and my parents had survived?

Sometimes strolling hand in hand with Simon, sometimes on my own, with him waiting at an exit, we didn't speak the whole time. That's how it is at Yad Vashem—silent. Except for the internal conversations. Don't worry, Mama, I'm here, I'm looking for the Afikomen and I'll find it.

The visit brought me peace and strength. After that immersion into ugliness and brutality, emerging outside onto the Judean hillside brimming with modern Israel was an epiphany of hope and survival against all odds. Like me, like all of us who escaped Hitler's grip.

Chapter 16

THE LETTER UNDER my door could have been torn from the pages of *Der Stürmer*, the vitriolic Nazi rag. Illustrated with caricatures of hook-nose medieval money-lenders defiling a maiden and the upheld hand of an Israeli stop sign, the garish assemblage of cut-out letters spelled out, "You have been warned, Lily Kovner. Stop or else."

"Well, they certainly get an 'A' for creativity," I said to Simon as we read this missive in the kitchen of my flat. "Taking the art of the threat to a new level."

"You see what this means, don't you, Lily. The anti-Semitic cartoons, the Nazi slant? There may be a connection here to something like the Odessa organization of old Nazis."

"Or maybe just creative license," I said. "You sound like Uncle, who brought that up, too. What would they have to do with an object like a Seder plate? Why would they care? Do you think there's a secret stash of gold inside it or some other prized antique writing, like a lost epistle of a saint?"

He laughed. "Now who's getting creative?"

I pushed the letter aside. "Not exactly a note to stuff into the Wailing Wall. Let's forget it, and enjoy Shabbat. With the Mossad on my side, I'm not going to worry. Though it reminds me both why I'm here and how nice it was to get away from it the past twenty-four hours."

I hugged Simon tightly and responded to his kiss. "Can you stay?"

He nodded. I moved my head back to say, "Even through tomorrow? I'd love to have you meet my family."

"I don't have to go back to Tel Aviv until Sunday morning. And I brought a bag with me."

"I know—I saw you putting it in the trunk when you didn't think I was watching."

"Sneaky reporter," he said. "Ok, now that my staying is settled, I want to help you with tomorrow's lunch as much as I can. But, first, there's something that I like to do whenever I'm in Jerusalem for Shabbat. Go to the Wall for sundown. Not with the note you just received, of course."

The famous Western or Wailing Wall in the Old City of Jerusalem is an easy walk from Rehavia, so Simon and I strolled hand in hand, along with the throngs making the trek to the Jaffa Gate and through the maze of the Old City to the Western Wall plaza. Emerging from the security checkpoint overlooking a sea of black hats, Simon pulled out a small velvet case from which he withdrew a prayer shawl and *kippah*. I tied the silk scarf at my neck around my head.

"Very Jackie O," he said.

"Right! Only if she were in *Fiddler on the Roof*."

Then we headed to our designated gender areas. I always resent the demotion to the smaller women's side. It is one reason why, I must confess, the Wall doesn't do much for me spiritually. The crowds and the sidelong glances of the observant women annoy me. Even though I always dress respectfully in a long black skirt kept in my Jerusalem flat for these occasions, I sense that they know I'm not one of them and look down on me because of it.

My spirituality and religious practice don't derive from unquestioning adherence to every word of Torah. That could be another reason why visiting the Wall doesn't touch me as it does others. While I rejoiced that Israel regained it, I question that the Wall is a remnant of the Temple. But, just as I don't cast aspersions on those who believe it, I don't want them to think of me as a lesser Jew because I don't. To Hitler we were all the same. Even women.

Glancing toward the crowd on my left, I saw Simon talking to a man, also draped in a *tallit*, who looked familiar. It took me a minute to place him as Avi, the agent I met in the market. A little Mossad business at the Wall? Why should that surprise me? Probably a daily occurrence.

As we walked back to the flat, I noticed an observant woman who looked just like the one I'd seen at the market probing cucumbers. She leaned against an old Fiat, smoking. When she saw Simon and me coming, she slipped into the car and drove away.

I said, "Did you see that?"

"What?"

"That religious woman. She was smoking and she got into the car and drove away. It's already Shabbat. Why would she drive?"

"Oh, her," he said. "That's Shulamit. She's not really observant."

"Another Mossad contact?"

"Yes. They've been watching your building."

"It's shameful for her to disguise herself as *dati*," I said.

"Don't you remember the story of how Golda Meir dressed up as an Arab woman to meet with the king of Transjordan? This isn't Halloween. They need to do what gets the job done."

As he and I did in the next hour to wind up with a Shabbat dinner of thyme-roasted chicken, couscous, and a salad made from cucumber, tomato, onion, and mint. A large pot of vegetables transforming to gvetch simmered on the stove for the next day's lunch. In the background Ella Fitzgerald sang Gershwin.

Later, as we lay in each other's arms, I asked whether, when he was here, the guard was called off.

"Are you my surveillance?"

"Not officially. They're on it. Don't worry."

Shabbat morning dawned with sunlight streaming through the branches outside into the bedroom. I awoke to the sound of puttering in the kitchen and the smell of coffee. A steaming cup personally delivered to me in bed was something I could get used to.

"Good morning," said the smiling coffee guy, settling himself next to me with his own cup. "Now, tell me, who's Aunt Lottie again?"

"Lottie Koopman. From the diamond business. My mother's older sister who raised me in London from the age of nine. She was six or seven years older than my mother and Uncle Erich, who were twins. You said you knew them. Arnold was her husband."

"Got it," said Simon. "So, she's Julian's and Daniel's mother."

"Right. As a matter of fact, Daniel and his wife, Hannah, are here, too, from London, and they're coming. Aunt Lottie spends several months a year in Tel Aviv. She's ninety-three and still going strong—very with it—but someone usually flies back and forth with her. She may be going back with them for Passover."

"And your newfound cousin, Ruth, is also coming, with her husband and kids?"

"I'm so excited about that—and to have all of us together. It was such a source of frustration to Aunt Lottie to lose contact with Uncle Erich after we heard he'd survived the war. I'm sure this will be very emotional for her. I probably should have called her, or Daniel, to warn them."

"She doesn't sound like the type who's going to pass out from shock," said Simon. "I find that older people who've made it so long in good shape have a built-in cushion for the unexpected—both good and bad. It's resilience."

"And survival instinct. Uncle, too."

Four hours later, when my aunt arrived, I introduced Simon as a friend.

"Friend? Just like Elisabeth and Nachman," said my nonagenarian aunt. "They should have gotten married. My mother was such a bitch."

"Mum, that's ancient history," my cousin, Daniel, said. "Sorry, Simon, she's a pip. Always has been, I'm afraid."

His wife, Hannah, just rolled her eyes.

Simon laughed. "Obviously, Lily inherited that gene."

Daniel explained to his mother that Simon was in the jewelry trade in New York and they knew each other from the diamond industry.

My cousin said, "Are you in Israel on business, Simon?"

"Originally, yes, but pleasure, too, now that I've been able to spend some time with your cousin. Helping out her hunt for Afikomen."

"What?" Aunt Lottie jumped in. "The Afikomen? It's not even Pesach yet. And, aren't you a little old to be hunting for the Afikomen, dear?"

"It's a silly code name I've given to my search for the Italian Seder plate that the Nazis stole. Do you remember, Auntie, that blue glass and silver piece?"

"That Nachman brought your mother the last time we were all together? There was such fighting that night about the Nazis, about leaving Austria. That was the very last time I saw any of them, except you and Nachman. All of a sudden you're looking for that Seder plate? Why?"

"I saw it at a Judaica auction in New York. The auction house withdrew it, after I made a fuss, and I think it's here in Israel."

Daniel said, "But weren't you just in London, Lily? Last week when we came here? Julian and Ella talked to Elizabeth when they got back on Thursday, and she said you'd just left for Israel. What were you doing there?"

"I was there to meet Helen Wolf, who was a consultant to Jews seeking long lost looted works of art."

"I heard Helen Wolf speak a few weeks ago," Hannah said, "What do you mean 'was'?"

"She died just before I got to her flat. I found her body, as a matter of fact."

"How ghastly," said Aunt Lottie.

Hannah looked mystified. "My cousin, Rose, who knew her as a girl in Glasgow, was with me and mentioned that Helen had been sick, but was doing fine. Her death must have been very sudden."

"Yes. Very," said Simon, signaling me to end this conversation.

"Listen, everyone," I said, "we have other guests coming. I'd wanted to make it a complete surprise, but some preparation could be a good idea. The other day I met Uncle Erich's daughter. She lives here, is married with twin children, and they're all coming for lunch any minute."

Aunt Lottie cried out, "Oh, my God," and everyone rushed to her side to make sure she was okay. "Erich's daughter? My brother's daughter? Lily, I don't understand. We never heard from him after the Communists took over China. He had a daughter?"

Daniel said, "Don't you remember, Mum, that we knew he'd married and they couldn't leave just then because his wife was pregnant with complications? I can scarcely believe I remember it, to be honest."

"Erich passed away years ago. His daughter's name now is Ruth," I said. "She's an art historian who works at Mosaica, the house that tried to auction off the Seder plate. In fact, she's helped me get an appointment tomorrow with a key figure in my search."

"Ruth," Aunt Lottie said. "Not a very Chinese name."

"She took it, Auntie, when she converted to Judaism, after the biblical Ruth. Her husband's name is Boaz, and his mother's named Naomi. Just like in the Bible."

At that moment the buzzer rang, and we all heard the pounding of the footsteps on the stairs. I opened the door, and there was my stunning cousin who hugged me and introduced Boaz, a lean, graying six-footer, and Eli and Talia, both fair with dark black hair and tall for ten.

Almost on cue, they held out their hands and said, "Shalom, Cousin Lily."

Everyone jabbered and laughed as introductions were made all around. Aunt Lottie hugged a crouched down Ruth and then Boaz and the twins and wept for at least ten minutes. By the time we sat down for lunch, one wouldn't have known that this was a reunion of family members who had just learned of one another's existence.

Simon blended right in, telling stories to the children, helping me serve, and graciously accepting compliments on the gvetch while toasting me as hostess and cook of the poached fish, salads, kugel, cheeses, fruit, and cake that went with it.

"I'm curious, Ruth," he asked, "how long have you worked at Mosaica?"

"About four years. It's been real learning experience seeing the business of Judaica marketplace. I'm academic at heart, but not a lot of university positions in Israel. Nor many galleries or auction houses either with real McCoy, as you'd say, real antiques. Mostly in Israel you see contemporary designs or religious items new made to look old. No pedigree."

"You know," Simon said, "until the auction where I met Lily, I don't remember ever seeing Mosaica hold a public sale in New York. I'd seen their catalogue and had been to the gallery here. I didn't even know until recently that you've got an office in Manhattan."

"Eliezer Ben-Shuvah, owner, has made strategic decision to gain foothold in New York. He's seen Sotheby's and Christie's do well in Judaica. Now, with opening of former Soviet Union, there's greater flow of merchandise that hadn't come to market before."

The premise of my magazine assignment, I thought. The angle my editor, Marty, wanted that I wasn't pursuing. Something to worry about later.

"Globalization," said Daniel. "The buzz word of 1990. China is on everyone's radar these days in that connection, though not in Judaica, obviously. Have you been back there, Ruth?"

"Yes. Boaz had conference last summer, and we all went. It was odd time to be in Beijing, only six weeks after Tiananmen, but we spent four days in Shanghai, which was wonderful. The city is changing, but I could still find my way around."

"Do you have any relatives left on your mother's side?" I asked.

"Just one aunt and uncle in Shanghai and their daughter who's married and has one son. Two other uncles and their families escaped to Hong Kong during revolution. We had wonderful reunion there. Just like today."

Around four o'clock Ruth and Boaz gathered Eli and Talia to say their good-byes and exchanged phone numbers and addresses with Aunt Lottie and Daniel.

"We have to stop to see Boaz's parents before we go back to Tel Aviv," Ruth said. "They live in French Hill. But I'll drive in again tomorrow, Lily, for lunch with Shaul. The King David at noon. I have booked table in my name. This has been so wonderful. Can't begin to thank you. I only hope that we can find Seder plate."

I hugged her and said, "If nothing else, it's brought us together, a tremendous victory."

Twenty minutes later Simon and I helped Daniel and Hannah maneuver Aunt Lottie down the stairs and out to their car. As they drove away, I saw a woman wearing baggy painter's pants, a black leather bomber jacket, and an oversized newsboy's cap standing across the street up the block. When our eyes met, she quickly turned her head away and walked in the opposite direction toward Ramban Street.

"That's her," I said to Simon.

"Who?"

"That's the woman from London, the woman who was leaving Helen Wolf's building when I got there. Her outfit is different, but the way she has that cap cocked to hide her eyes, that's how she had her rain hat. With just a little blonde hair showing. She looks like Marlene Dietrich in *Witness for the Prosecution.*"

He laughed. "Is that what you told Scotland Yard?"

"I think so."

"No wonder you were a suspect," he said. "The outfit that this one is wearing is not exactly Marlene's style."

"To throw me off the track," I said. "I don't know why and I don't know who she is, but that woman was in London and now she's here. If your Mossad buddy, Avi, really thinks Helen Wolf was murdered, she's the killer."

"Okay, I'll get him on the phone as soon as we get back inside."

I described her to Avi, who had heard the same information from Sam in London.

"I don't understand how she got into Israel," he said. "We have had people posted since we heard about Helen Wolf and knew that you were coming. We had a sketch and a telescopic photo from Sam, and we've closely scrutinized women in the arrivals hall at Ben-Gurion Airport and their passports for days."

"Maybe she disguised herself, or maybe this is a disguise," I said.

"You're good, Mrs. Kovner, very good," said Avi, who didn't strike me as a man normally generous with compliments.

"Come on," said Simon, as I hung up the phone and realized that he had single-handedly almost polished off cleaning up from lunch, "let's finish the dishes and relax," nodding toward the bedroom. "It's a double mitzvah on Shabbat, you know."

Making love was one precept of observance I was happy to follow. For someone who had had such a long draught, I was certainly making up for lost time. My comfort level with Simon had increased so much that I nearly forgot we'd only known each other for less than two weeks. Sharing my family gathering, including the preparation and the aftermath, intensified the intimacy and, if possible, heightened the reward of our lovemaking.

By the time we awoke from our nap, it was dark.

"It's Saturday night," Simon said, running his fingers along my spine while mine tripped combed down from his hairy chest to his penis. "We could stay in bed all evening or go out. Two good options, but, as great as the first is, I think getting out on the town would be fun. We'll still have this to come back to. What do you think?"

"Out on the town in Jerusalem? Isn't that an oxymoron? It's pretty quiet here, compared to Tel Aviv."

"Nonsense. There's a great jazz place I know, some good restaurants. Not that I'm particularly hungry after that huge lunch, but we might want a snack later."

"And we did have a lot of exercise. Okay, let's get up and go out."

I never would have found the dive in the Old Katamon neighborhood. From the sidewalk we navigated down a narrow stairway of cobblestones to a subterranean hovel. Ten small round tables with rickety wooden chairs, scratched and splintered, were jammed together on top of stained and tattered oriental rugs. Smoke from tobacco and marijuana hung in the air and mixed with incense to give the place a fragrance that reminded me of Berkeley in 1968.

A genial man with a salt-and-pepper beard showed us to a table in front of the stage. After plunking two glasses of red wine in front of us, he sat down at a battered upright piano. Then a thin, frail looking man carrying a clarinet emerged from behind a curtain made from a blanket.

"That's Harold Rubin," said Simon. "He's fantastic. Came here from South Africa years ago. Also paints. Wait until you hear him."

He was right. If I'd closed my eyes, I would have thought it was Artie Shaw playing. Nonstop for ninety minutes Rubin and the pianist performed a set that ranged from the familiar, like "Begin the Beguine," to original arrangements that melded Middle Eastern and African strains with classical jazz.

"That was incredible," I said, as we strolled back to Simon's car afterward.

"A real change of pace, for sure. I'm glad you enjoyed it. Are you hungry, Lily?"

"I'm sure I could eat," I said, "although it's late, and tomorrow's a big day. We do have leftovers at home."

Raiding the refrigerator together, nibbling on cold chicken, picking at a last square of kugel, slathering a little gvetch on challah bread—a cozy late night nosh that made me feel like we'd been together forever.

Chapter 17

THE NEXT MORNING, Sunday, was a workday in Israel, and Simon had to leave by eight for a staff meeting at his Tel Aviv office.

"I wish I could stay and meet Rotan with you," he said, after he had gathered up his belongings and stood in the kitchen with my face cupped in his hands. "And I really don't want to leave you, period."

"I don't want you to, either. It's been a wonderful few days."

"You must promise to call me as soon as you know something. I'll be in the office most of the day but I'll drive back here tonight."

I stepped into the dining room of the King David at 11:58. The maître d', when I asked for the Sofer table, said that Mrs. Sofer had phoned to say that she'd been delayed by a meeting but her guests should start without her, even order lunch; she hoped to arrive within a half-hour. Though he showed me to a table that afforded the classic view of the Old City walls, I chose to sit with my back to it, the better to witness Rotan's arrival.

He entered the dining room just as the maître d' returned to his station and obviously delivered Ruth's message while leading the professor to the table. Abruptly stopping short of his destination and visibly blanching at the sight of his prospective lunch companion, Rotan recovered sufficiently to thank his escort and nod silently as he took a seat across from me. Ruth was right. His dignity would preclude a messy scene in public. Just having him at the table was a victory.

"Professor Rotan," I said.

"It's Mrs. Kovner, isn't it? Are you and Ruth Sofer really so deluded as to have me believe that the two of you are cousins?"

"I can understand your disbelief, but, yes, we are first cousins. Her father was my mother's twin brother, the uncle whom the family had lost touch with after the Communists came to power in China. It's very exciting for both of us and for the rest of the family that we've found one another after all these years."

Rotan's eyes widened, his body language loosening slightly, but he remained silent.

"But you know why I wanted to meet with you, don't you, Mr. Rothenberg?"

Obviously rattled, he whispered, "How do you know that name?"

"Stefan Rothenberg, that was your name in Germany, your name before Israel, isn't that so?"

"Yes, and who cares? It's hardly a crime here to have changed your name to something more modern. Look at David Ben-Gurion, Moshe Dayan, Golda Meir. We all changed our names."

"Nobody's accusing you of a crime, professor. But I know that Stefan Rothenberg was at university with Helen Wolf, with Rudolf Bucholz, and maybe with Eliezer Ben-Shuvah, although there's no record of him at Cambridge, or even of someone Jewish who might have also changed his name to something like Ben-Shuvah."

I whipped out the photo that I'd swiped from Helen Wolf's flat and plunked it down in front of the professor.

"This is you with Helen and Rudolf Bucholz at Cambridge, isn't it? Bucholz was the Nazi officer who looted my home in 1938 and took that di Salamone Seder plate. He also took my father—to Dachau. I never saw my father again."

Just then the waiter approached to take our order. Rotan asked for a brandy. I ordered a chicken sandwich and hot tea. After the waiter's retreat, the professor looked around the nearly empty dining room, sighed, and finally spoke.

"All right, Mrs. Kovner, you win. I will tell you the whole story. You won't like it, I don't like it, but it is what it is, and the time has come to make a clean breast of it and be done."

Rotan's drink arrived. He took a sip, sighed again, and breathed deeply, as if he were about to dive off a cliff.

"We were friends, Rudi, Helen, me, all of us; Rudi and I who came from Germany, Helen a Scot. Rudi wasn't an anti-Semite then, if you can believe it. He would have stayed in England after we finished up at Cambridge, but his father wouldn't allow it. The father was a banker in Munich, Karl Bucholz, a big shot from an old family, the type who years before wouldn't have let Hitler shine his shoes. But he bought into the shame of Versailles, the degradation that the First War had brought unto Germany. So, when Hitler and his goons came calling for money to finance the new Reich, old man Bucholz said it would be an honor."

The Cambridge connection. I was right about that. Rotan was opening up. What a wonderful mitzvah Ruth had performed in arranging this meeting.

"Rudi's mother came from Italy. Her father was Mussolini's personal physician. She died young, when we were students, but Rudi attributed his sensitivity to art and culture to the Italian side of the family."

"Sensitivity? Ask the people of Rohatyn about that," I said.

"He wasn't like that at university," he said. "In fact, one year, I think it was 1935, he sat me down at a pub and told me point blank not to return home for the winter holidays. The Nuremburg Laws had just been enacted. My parents belonged to the 'it will blow over' school of Jews—all the way to Buchenwald. Rudy saved my life. Instead of Germany, I came here that December and started the process to obtain a Palestine passport. I begged my parents to leave Germany with my younger brother. But they wouldn't. They came for a visit one summer and went back horrified by the heat, the dust, the Arabs.

He gulped more brandy and signaled the waiter for another.

"Years passed, World War II. I fought alongside the British in the Palestine Brigade. I grew to love this land and became an ardent Zionist. Rudi, well, you know what he became. Helen . . ."

"Helen worked with the Monuments Men sorting art in Germany," I said.

"Yes. I ran into her in Germany after the war. I had the art training, too, of course, but they didn't recruit Monuments Men from the Palestine Brigade. I worked in the Bricha to help refugees come here from Europe and also to smuggle in arms and other materiel for the bloody battle we knew we'd have when statehood was declared. This was when the British were doing everything in their power to keep Jews and guns blockaded from our shores.

"When I ran into Helen, we went out one night and started talking about old times. Through her work with art, she'd already learned about Rudi's role in looting, which upset her tremendously. I gave her the additional news that our friend had gained the moniker, 'butcher of Rohatyn.' She wept when I told her about the massacre. Then she told me she and Rudi had been lovers at Cambridge, enough in love that he wanted to stay in England to marry her. I can only imagine how his father reacted to that—a Jewish woman, no less. Helen's family was equally appalled. Funny, I never suspected back at Cambridge. We were all so much more discreet then, of course."

My chicken sandwich arrived. Watching the professor inhale brandy, I decided to order a glass of white wine. "Go on," I said, when the waiter had retreated again.

"No one knew where Rudi was after the war. His last posting had been Italy. He was reported to have been on leave when the war ended."

"This I know from Simon Wiesenthal's files," I said.

The professor shrugged and took another deep breath.

"I was in Rome in early 1947, in March, almost two years after the war ended. I got a note from someone named Guido Morelli that he had information that would help my work on behalf of the Zionists. He proposed meeting at a ratty bar in Trastevere, near the old ghetto. When I got there, this Morelli turned out to be Rudi, much thinner and dressed like a laborer, just a guy on the street in Rome stopping to meet a friend for a drink."

I took a sip of the wine that had just arrived. The professor blotted his forehead with a cotton handkerchief.

"You know what it was like in Europe then," he said.

"I only know how it was in London—cold and austere."

Rotan said, "You'd see people running into each other, amazed to find friends still alive. Rudi greeted me like that. You'd have thought we were long-lost brothers. We sat down, and he ordered the most expensive wine on the list, which made the proprietor rejoice, considering we were the only customers.

"As we sat drinking wine, Rudi—he insisted I call him Guido—laid out a fantastic proposal, that he could lead us, the Zionists, to a cache of guns and other equipment in a hidden warehouse in northern Italy. What he wanted in return was for us to get him out of Europe with a new identity, with papers to settle somewhere else."

My jaw dropped. "Unbelievable," was all I could say.

"I told you it was fantastic. Fantasy, in fact," he said. "I told him I couldn't imagine such a bargain being struck and, anyway, I lacked the authority to approve or reject such a scheme. He begged me to at least take it to my superiors. Two of them were in town at the time. I said I would but did not hold out any expectation that they would do anything other than laugh me out of the room, with such a ridiculous proposal. Rudi said I could let him know by returning to this bar at the same time three days later. If I didn't show up, he would approach the Arabs.

"The next morning I presented his request. To my surprise—no, to my shock—these gentlemen didn't give me a flat no. Instead, they said they'd figure it out and get back to me that night. I walked around Rome all that day—it was my first time there—amid the rubble alongside the historic ruins. Despite the damage from the war, it was so beautiful. The vistas. The Sistine Chapel. Wonderland for an art historian. But I felt hollow, stunned that the leaders I respected would even consider such a deal."

"So, it happened," I said.

"Yes. When I returned to their hotel suite that night, they told me that I was to arrange to pick up the arms and, if it all checked out, to take Rudi to a house in Florence, where he could be safeguarded until we could transport him out of Italy. They were actually planning to smuggle him out with a boatload of Jews. This I objected to vehemently. 'What if someone recognizes him?' I asked. Mutiny could have broken out on the boat. These journeys were risky enough without the possibility of provocation like an ex-Nazi on board.

"'Never mind,' they said, 'we'll make sure that won't happen. No one will recognize him. If he is, justice will be done. We need arms. This is a small price to pay. He came to us for a new identity, he'll get one—as a Jew.'"

Rotan paused for a moment and beckoned the waiter for some mineral water. He looked defeated, pathetic.

"Maybe you should eat something, professor," I said. My own untouched sandwich withered in front of me. "Order something, or take some of this." I pushed my plate toward him, and he picked up half the sandwich and took a bite.

"Thank you." He gulped a swig of water and continued.

"The day after I told Rudi we'd accepted his proposal, three colleagues and I went up north and met him at a monastery in the middle of the night.

Apparently, his cousin was one of the monks. Rudi had stayed there since he left his troops and went on leave just before the end of the war. With flashlights we tramped on the wet grass down a slope. There was a tunnel hollowed out of the ground which led to an enormous warehouse. Rudi said it had been there for centuries storing the skulls and bones of departed brethren, like Santa Catarina in the Sinai here. Also priceless Christian religious artifacts and other booty received as so-called donations. Rudi laughed in our faces. He said to us, 'You think we Germans were the master looters? We were amateurs compared to those old monks. And the popes, too.'"

"Was there any art there, or only guns?"

"Oh, there was art. I pointed my flashlight through the window of a door to another room and saw a Picasso and a small Braques. I remember, because it was what Hitler called degenerate art. But that wasn't what we came for. We needed the rifles, machine guns, ammunition, grenades, dynamite, machine parts, field glasses that were on the shelves, and what was in the middle—a jeep, drivable, with the German insignia painted out. It was a warrior's treasure trove. We'd brought three trucks and were barely able to stuff it all, and Rudi, into them."

"Why didn't you just take it and shoot him?"

"Believe me, I thought about it. But Rudi brought a posse of a couple of monks, including his cousin—they would have been no problem—and six thugs with their own machine guns. When I saw them, I thought it was a trap and we'd be ambushed. Maybe that would have been better." His voice trailed off.

"But you went through with the deal," I said.

"Yes. We took Rudi to Florence. We had a doctor there who did some surgery, changed his eyelids and chin. You know he'd always looked more Italian than German anyway, not exactly the Aryan ideal, so passing him off as Jewish wasn't that hard. He'd lost his bulk, like all of the refugees, and we didn't try to beef him up. Our doctor had thorough instructions that included branding his arm with a camp number and circumcising him. These procedures he performed with particular relish; he'd lost his parents and wife in Auschwitz. There was no anesthesia."

"I wonder where Ruth is," I said, looking at the door of the dining room.

"Just as well she doesn't hear this, though she will know soon enough."

"Why is that?"

"We gave Rudi the name Eliezer Ben-Shuvah. Ben-Shuvah, the son of return, it means in Hebrew. Ruth works for him. He owns Mosaica."

I must have suspected something as incredible as this had happened, because it didn't really shock me. But I felt enormous relief, validation, and satisfaction to finally hear this. It explained everything.

"So, Bucholz and Ben-Shuvah are one in the same," I said. "Bucholz got to Israel and stayed?"

Rotan nodded. Before he could speak again, the waiter approached the table and handed me a note that said Mrs. Sofer had called again. There had been an accident on the road, and traffic to Jerusalem was blocked from the airport exit to Mod'in. She'd turned back to Tel Aviv, and she'd talk to me later. I handed the note to Rotan.

"As I said, she'll know soon enough."

"So, Bucholz, now Ben-Shuvah, he's been here all these years?"

"Yes," Rotan said. "As luck would have it, his crossing proved uneventful. Foul weather made most of the passengers too sick to get acquainted with strangers and threw off the British patrols that usually hovered off the ports. Fog and rain in Haifa obscured the Haganah welcoming party that swiftly got everyone off the boat and transported to safe houses throughout the city.

"Not only was Rudi not recognized, but he'd won praise from the crew and passengers for helping the captain when the first mate slipped and almost fell overboard in a storm. I'm sure he expected his return to Zion would only be a way station before he could go somewhere else, but he asked us for a lift, and where else could we take him? So, Ben-Shuvah dug in, literally, on a kibbutz in the Galilee. And fell in love with Yehudit, the girl who had piloted the dinghy that ferried him from the ship to shore. They married, had a son, Natan, who was killed in the Yom Kippur War, and a daughter, Yael, moved to Tel Aviv, where Mosaica opened in the 1960s."

"I've met Yael," I said.

"Yes, she works in the business."

"Why did he go into Judaica, rather than some other field of art?"

"There was no market here for Picasso or any fancy artists then. Times were tough in Israel for many years. Rudi determined that Judaica would sell and also that people who needed money had it to auction off."

"So, it wasn't all looted?"

"To be honest, Mrs. Kovner, until you came into the picture, I didn't know that any of it was looted."

"Or didn't want to know," I said. "But you stayed involved with him. You'd seen all that stuff in Italy. Didn't you ever think that he'd gotten it out and brought it here to sell? Come on, professor."

He fiddled with a breadcrumb on the tablecloth.

"I don't know what I thought. It was a business arrangement. We hadn't seen each other for many years before he started Mosaica. He came to see me at the university one day and told me he wanted to open an art business, a gallery and auction house, and needed backers. He said he would take care of me, if I could find some people to invest in this. I didn't want to, I'd tried to forget the whole thing, forget him, but he offered me a lot of money, if the business succeeded, and I have a brother . . ."

Rotan started to cry. As much as I wanted to press him, I waited until he'd composed himself.

"I have a brother, Mrs. Kovner," he said. "Manfred. Dr. Mengele thought he was a perfect specimen. Seventeen when they met. I didn't even know Manfred had survived until the summer of 1946. Not that you'd call it life. He doesn't speak. He can't walk. When I found him in a British army hospital in Germany, I had to leave him there. There was no way he could travel during the Bricha, with the British lurking about. I brought him here after the War of Independence. He stays in a good facility in Karmiel up north. My point in telling you this is that I needed money to take care of him. So, I helped Rudi start the business, found a silent investor, someone I knew from the old days, one of the Zionist leaders who had approved the scheme."

I couldn't bear to ask the next question. I didn't have to.

"Nachman Tanski was the original partner in Mosaica," Rotan said. "I know about your relationship. He called me after the auction, the first time I'd heard from him in years."

This was a blow like the sight of the Seder plate on that stage. Sweat broke out on my forehead, and my chest tightened. I reached for my water glass and started to cry. Rotan leaned over and touched my other hand.

"I know it's a shock. But, if it's any comfort to you, Tanski doesn't have anything to do with Mosaica now. Rudi, I mean Eliezer, paid back his investment and a nice profit years ago."

"But he approved the original deal with the devil? Did Bucholz, Ben-Shuvah, blackmail the two of you into helping him go into business?"

"Blackmail is an ugly word," he said. "I wouldn't say that."

"Everything about this is ugly," I said. "Okay, professor, now that you've told me all this, where's my Seder plate?"

"I brought it back from New York. When I called Eliezer to tell him what had happened, he told me to bring it to Tel Aviv, to the gallery, but to leave it in my car. We met in his office, then he got it out and transferred it to his car. He knew you'd gotten a search warrant in New York. He figured you'd eventually come to the gallery in Israel. Where it is now I don't know. That's the truth."

"And what about all the threats I've had? And Helen Wolf? Do you know I went to see her in London and found her dead? Although the coroners in London said she died of natural causes, she may have been murdered. Is Ben-Shuvah, Bucholz, behind all this? Did he have her killed?"

Now Rotan looked shocked. "I know nothing about any of that, truly, Mrs. Kovner."

I looked at my watch, it was one-thirty. In the past few minutes fifty years of love and trust had been turned upside down. I rose, looked down at Rotan, who'd become a pitifully shrunken old man.

"I have to leave. Now," I said.

The check would be his problem.

I rushed out of the King David and walked back to the flat in a record eight minutes. I noticed Shulamit, wearing tight jeans and a brown leather jacket instead of modest Orthodox garb, smoking against a tree in front just as I arrived. I raced up the steps and put my key in the lock. At that moment one black-gloved hand reached around my neck from the right while another pulled my left arm downward, nearly out of its socket.

"Help," I screamed.

"You haven't learned, Mrs. Kovner; we tried to warn you," said the same raspy voice I'd heard on the phone.

I struggled to turn around to see her face, but my assailant kept my neck taut. My feet were free, though, and I pushed one backward, striking her shin. Years of the flutter kick paid off. The pain loosened her grip long enough for me to turn my head and see the blonde from London, this time wearing a felt cloche pulled down to her eyes. She did have quite a hat collection.

Instantly, the sound of boots on the steps and a yell of "Mrs. Kovner" brought Shulamit. The blonde grasped me as tightly as she could, but I was able to slam my elbow into her solar plexus. This slackened her grip, just as Shulamit came running around the corner pointing a gun at us.

My assailant let go of me and put up her hands. When Shulamit reached for the hat to expose the face, she pulled a blonde wig off, too. This revealed the raven haired daughter of Ben-Shuvah. In another few seconds a crackling walkie-talkie signaled the arrival of Avi. By this time I'd opened the door of my flat and sat down. Shulamit had handcuffed Yael and stood next to her just inside the doorway.

Avi came in and asked if I was all right.

"Yes, yes," I said. "Fine. But I need to get to Tel Aviv."

"My father doesn't have your Seder plate, bitch," the charming Miss Ben-Shuvah screamed. "You're wasting your time. You and that Helen Wolf. You just had to come along and ruin his life. Our family's life. She couldn't leave well enough alone, either, trying to expose his past. He's made up for his past."

"Shut up," said Shulamit.

"No," Avi said, "let her talk. She's digging her own grave. Mrs. Kovner, is this the woman you saw leaving Helen Wolf's flat in London?"

"Yes."

"You know what the lazy, underpaid coroners in London said? That she died of an accidental self-administered dose of morphine. They didn't bother to look for the tiny prick of a needle that this one stuck into her."

Turning to Yael, he said, "You're an Israeli. Why does it surprise you that the Mossad has someone in position to make a more thorough examination, even in London?"

It surprised *me*, but there was no time to dwell on it.

"I need to make a quick phone call," I said, "and then I want to leave for Tel Aviv to find out what her father did with the Seder plate."

Avi motioned for Shulamit to leave with Yael. "I will drive you to Tel Aviv," he said.

When I heard Bernice, Uncle's housekeeper, answer, I asked to speak to him.

"Why, he left for Israel, Miss Lily," she said. "Last night. He should be getting to his house any minute now. He called that Bella woman," his Israeli housekeeper, "to get it ready. I'm sure you'll hear from him tonight. He wanted to surprise you, just decided yesterday to pick up and go. Wasn't feeling too well, but he insisted on going. His nephew, Bob, flew over with him, thank the Lord."

I hung up, wondering if he was coming because he knew I would find out about him and Bucholz. My head throbbed, and my neck ached. Between the interview with Rotan and the encounter with Yael, I would have gladly laid down with ice and aspirin. But there would be time for that later. If only Simon were with me. However, I'd come this far on my own and I'd manage the next step, too.

Chapter 18

Driving into Tel Aviv, Avi told me that the Mossad, along with police in Israel, Europe, and the United States, had suspected for years that Ben-Shuvah's business dealings were less than kosher.

"We only thought he was dealing in fake manuscripts," he said. "That's Simon's department."

"Simon's department? What are you talking about? Is Simon one of you? A Mossad agent?"

"Yes. That's what he was doing at the auction the day you met him. He's been on this case for years."

"But he's a businessman in New York."

"Great cover, don't you think? He's very specialized, only works for us in that one narrow area. Old Jewish manuscripts are his passion, and he knows them cold. Occasionally, he gives us a tip or two on something else. Like your Seder plate. Looted art. But we never thought it would lead to a Nazi war criminal, never really had an inkling until you had lunch with Professor Rotan today."

All this information whirled in my head in as much of a jumble as the scenery whizzing by along Highway 1. Avi drove in typically Israeli fashion, at high speed, weaving in and out of lanes around other cars.

"Are you serious? Was our table bugged?"

"I hope the service in the King David dining room was satisfactory, madam," he said.

"So, now what's going to happen when we get to Mosaica? I still don't know where the Seder plate is. Won't Ben-Shuvah know that Rotan tipped me off? And what about Yael?"

"We picked up the professor right after you left. Actually, after he paid the check. His first words were, 'Didn't I leave enough of a tip?' So, he didn't have time for any phone calls to Tel Aviv. As for Yael, we still don't know if her father put her up to all her shenanigans, including the threats to you and probably Helen Wolf's murder. But she obviously knew about her father's past and wanted to protect him and the family."

"And Nachman Tanski—the original deal and his financing of Mosaica? What will happen to him?"

"Nachman Tanski is a hero in Israel. A respected founder and philanthropist."

"And ninety-six years old."

"And ninety-six years old."

My earlier conversations with Avi had been so hurried that I hadn't noticed that he didn't sound like a *sabra*, a native-born Israeli. His English lacked the scrambled syntax and gutteral Rs of someone whose first language was Hebrew.

"Where are you from, Avi?"

"England."

"I thought so. What part?"

"Suburbs north of London. Lots of Jews there."

"When did you make aliyah?"

"When I was eighteen, just after Suez, in 1956. I wasn't cut out for university. Couldn't stand the anti-Semitism in Britain. Came here, went into the Army, joined the Mossad right after they captured Eichmann. Everyone wanted to be one of them then. Married, had kids, the whole package."

"Do you have family left in England?"

"My mother died recently."

"I'm sorry. And your father?"

"Never met him. Died before I was born."

His clipped responses convinced me to stop asking personal questions. My thoughts turned to what would happen next. Would this be the final leg of Afikomen? I remembered that I hadn't called Simon after the meeting with Rotan. When would I see him again? Maybe the Mossad had alerted him to what was going on.

"Avi, does Simon know about what's happened today?"

"See for yourself," he said.

At that moment we pulled up to Mosaica, and there were Simon and a phalanx of three other men, including Sam from London, emerging from a white Mercedes station wagon. I was both happy and relieved to rush out of Avi's car straight into Simon's arms.

"I'm so glad you're all right," he said. "You had a brush with disaster. I never would have forgiven myself if something had happened to you. I should have stayed today, blown off my staff meeting, just cancelled."

"I'm fine," I said, "but I still don't have the Seder plate. And Uncle—I can't believe he was part of such a dastardly deal."

"One thing at a time, Lily," he said. "We'll see what happens inside here with Ben-Shuvah."

"You mean Bucholz," I said, after yet another kiss. "Hmm, you smell great, by the way." I'd just realized that there was no tobacco smell on his breath.

"I'm glad I pass your sniff test," he said. "Not one cigarette since I picked you up on Thursday. Didn't you notice that I didn't smoke the whole time we were together?"

"There was a lot to distract me," I said. "But it does make me happy."

"Let's go in, Simon, Mrs. Kovner—and Yitzchak." Avi motioned to a rock solid giant in the group that he should accompany us. "Sam, Moshe, and Amnon, you guys stand guard outside."

Framed by the black-and-white marble floor, white walls, and black leather furniture of the lobby, Ruth, with her alabaster skin and ebony hair, looked like part of the décor.

Alarmed by the entourage surrounding us, she said, "Lily, Simon. Who are these men?"

Avi flashed his Mossad identification. "Avi Ben-Ze'ev. We are here to see Mr. Ben-Shuvah. And you are?"

"Ruth Sofer. Lily's cousin. I work here, a curator. Lily, what's happened? How was your lunch with Shaul?"

I whispered to her, "It's a long story. You're about to find out. Your boss is the Nazi war criminal who stole my Seder plate."

She gasped, turned even whiter, and nearly fainted, reaching for the huge potted ficus tree next to her before making her way to a rounded chair set into an alcove in a typically Bauhaus glass block wall. Unable to speak, she pointed the way to Ben-Shuvah's office. The Mossad contingent led the way down a corridor dotted with hanging glass cases containing small silver ritual items—kiddush cups, mezzuzahs, and the spice boxes and holders for the twisted candles used for the Havdalah service that ends Shabbat. I wondered how much of Mosaica's inventory was looted.

The old Nazi was standing behind his massive marble-topped desk. As Avi and Bucholz studied each other for an inexplicably long moment, something flashed into my head.

"Oh, my God," I said.

In the commotion involved in the Mossad agents positioning themselves around Ben-Shuvah, only Simon, standing in the back with me, heard.

"What's the matter?"

I pulled out the photo from Helen's flat and pointed to the image of the young Bucholz, then motioned to Simon to look at Avi's face. He read my mind and nodded.

I fished for Avi's business card and whispered, "Ben-Ze'ev, doesn't that mean son of Wolf?"

Simon's eyes widened, but he put a finger to his lips to signal silence just as Avi announced, "Eliezer Ben-Shuvah, alias Rudolf Bucholz, I have come to arrest you for crimes against humanity and for the theft of art, including this woman's Seder plate."

"I don't know what you're talking about," said Bucholz. "I have no alias. I am a rightful citizen of the State of Israel. And, as for your Seder plate, madam, it is not here, and I do not have it."

"The game is up, Bucholz," said Avi. "Your pal, Professor Rotan, has revealed everything, and we have your daughter in custody for the murder of Helen Wolf and the attempted murder of Mrs. Kovner. We know everything, except the whereabouts of the Seder plate."

"Rotan? That coward," Bucholz said. "But Yael? You have Yael? She killed Helen? Oh, my God, I never . . ."

Before our eyes he became an old broken man. He leaned heavily onto his desk and put his head in his hands. Recovering, he stood up and fiddled with the combination of the vault. Yitzchak helped him heave open the massive black metal door.

"See for yourselves," he said.

Simon and I filed through the opening and stepped gingerly into the vault. Inside were some gorgeous pieces, the likes of which I had only seen in museums or, years ago, at Uncle's: gold menorahs, jewel-topped Torah crowns, leather-bound volumes. But not my Seder plate.

As we came out facing Avi and Bucholz, it was like each of them was looking at a mirror. No wonder I thought Avi had looked familiar when I first met him in the market. I reached into my bag, pulled out the photo from Cambridge, and held it in front of the two of them.

"Where did you get that?" Avi said.

"At your . . . mother's," I said.

"That's you in this picture, isn't it?" Avi said to Bucholz. "Rotan said you knew my mother at Cambridge. But this is exactly how I looked thirty years ago."

"He's your father, Avi," I whispered.

"*Ya alah*," Avi swore in Arabic. "You're my father? I can't believe it. And your daughter, my half-sister, murdered my mother?"

"I loved your mother very much," Bucholz said. "But it never would have worked out for us, and we lost touch during the war. She wrote to me and sent me your baby pictures until September of 1939."

"How did you, or Yael, even know how to find her?" By now Avi was shouting.

"She was snooping around in her consulting work, writing me with questions about Mosaica, about my educational background, where I'd worked before I started the gallery, what I did during the war. I realized she knew who I was. Yael found out about Helen's inquiries and confronted me until I broke down and told her the truth. She's the only one in Israel who knows the truth; even my wife doesn't know. But I didn't tell Yael to kill Helen, I swear."

Ever the stalwart Mossad agent despite the shocking personal turn of events, Avi recovered his aplomb, took out handcuffs, and locked them around his father's wrists.

"Before we go, can you tell Mrs. Kovner where her Seder plate is?"

"At Nachman Tanski's house in Caesaria. I delivered it there this morning."

Somehow, I wasn't surprised.

"There's something I want to know," Simon said. "Why, and how, you held on to a Seder plate you looted as a Nazi officer."

"You, sir," Bucholz practically spat at Simon, "don't know much about the work of Abramo di Salamone. I am half-Italian and educated in the history of art from my country. I could spot a di Salamone a mile away when I saw it. Even with Hebrew writing, I treasured it from the first moment I saw it. I managed never to record it on the official lists and got it to my cousin's in Italy as soon as I could. Eventually, I had quite a nice collection at that monastery."

"So, I never would have found it on a Monuments Man inventory," I said.

"You all think Goering was the only collector of the Reich. He was just greedy, not a connoisseur of true value like me. And, believe me, plenty of others helped ourselves."

"If you treasured it so," Simon asked, "why were you auctioning the Seder plate off?"

"Cash flow problems. It would have fetched a tidy sum."

"The least of your problems now. Except for paying a good lawyer. In this country even a monster like you gets a defense. Democracy—sometimes I wish . . . " Avi mumbled in disgust.

The next moment Yitzchak the Giant shoved Bucholz toward the lobby and out, followed by Simon, Avi, and me. Avi stopped, leaned against a lobby wall, and dropped his head into his hands. I approached him and put a hand on his shoulder.

"Avi, I am so sorry," I said. "I feel responsible for your mother's death. If I hadn't started Afikomen, she would still be alive."

"No, Mrs. Kovner, you're not responsible. She was very ill. Who knows how much longer she had? But it's too bad you didn't get a chance to really meet her. You would have liked each other."

"I've caused so much upheaval," I said to Simon. "And still no Seder plate. But we both know where I have to go next."

"I'll drive you," he said.

After bidding farewell to Ruth, who tended to Avi with a chair and water, we headed north along the coast to Caesaria. It was already dark when we wound up the road that led to Uncle's villa. Older than Simon's and perched on a cliff, the sprawling house overlooked the sea and an excavated Roman amphitheatre. Bob Igra, his lawyer nephew, opened the door.

"Come in, Lily," he said.

I introduced Simon and said, "I need to see Uncle right away."

"I have bad news. Right after we got here he had a heart attack," Bob said. "He refuses to go to hospital, of course. He came because he wanted to surprise you and help out your search. You should go in to see him right away."

"Maybe I should stay here," said Simon. "Let you go alone."

"No need," I said. "Come with me."

We followed Bob into Uncle's bedroom. Facing his bed on a round table was the Seder plate.

As much as I had memorized what it looked like and imagined this moment, the splendor of the piece still amazed me. Even in the dim light of Uncle's bedside lamp, its highly polished silver radiated and the intricacy of its jeweled edges lent a textured richness to the simplicity of the clear royal blue shelves.

"It's remarkable," I heard Simon say.

Uncle turned his head from it to the door when he heard us coming and held out his arms. For the first time in over fifty years, I held back. He may have been sick but he sensed my conflict.

"You know, don't you? About Bucholz?"

"Yes, Uncle. I heard today. It's over. But how did the Seder plate get here?"

"I wanted to surprise you. I called that bastard and had him bring it here. I never knew he had it. Can you imagine, he kept it all those years? A Seder plate. That Nazi. I wanted to have a grand celebration, unveiling, dinner, the works. You know me, nothing I like better than a party."

"Shush, Uncle, get some rest. We'll celebrate when you feel better. We'll go home, have Passover with the kids, the Seder plate will be on the table for the first time since 1938."

In spite of myself, I leaned over and kissed his forehead. It was clammy. He reached up, took both of my arms, and pulled me close.

"Forgive me, Lily," he said. "I did it for Israel. Those times, you can't imagine, we were desperate. One makes decisions for a greater good. The odds were against us beating back the Arabs; no one wanted to help us. All those refugees still in Europe—they were still living in concentration camps, for God's sake, nowhere to go, just like before the war.

"Once Israel came about and we won the War of Independence, I forgot all about Bucholz. Until Rotan came to me about investing in the business. I didn't want everything to come out, so I did it. He'd made his life here as Ben-Shuvah, the son of return. I didn't want to be in the auction business. I hadn't given him or Mosaica a thought for twenty years—until you went to that auction two weeks ago."

Uncle struggled to breathe, yet persisted.

"I bought that Seder plate for your mother. That night, that Seder at your house, it was the last time I saw her. I never knew Ben-Shuvah had it. I'd have paid for it all over again—a hundred times more—to get it back for you."

"Rest, Uncle," I said. "Don't try to talk."

He smiled and held my arms tighter, then let go, and let his head fall back on the pillow. By the time I sat down next to his bed, his eyes had closed, and his breathing quickened to compensate for his slowing heart. From Arthur's last days in hospice care I knew this meant death was near. Ten minutes later I heard a loud gasp and one word, "Elisabeth," and then nothing.

EPILOGUE

Chapter 19

Two weeks later, on the first night of Passover, the Seder plate sat resplendent on the table in my New York apartment. Candlelight played like rain showers in sunlight upon its royal blue glass, silver, and jeweled edges, unfurling a rainbow on the white walls of my dining room.

My extended family sat around the table for the gala Seder. In addition to Elizabeth and Jonathan and Jacob and Amy and their twins, Ruth and Boaz, in the States for a conference, came with theirs. Simon brought his daughter, Jill.

Despite the age difference, the two sets of twins took off together hand in hand when it came time to look for the Afikomen, the real Afikomen—a piece of matzah wrapped in a napkin. Earlier the Israeli Eli and Talia had rattled off the Four Questions in Hebrew, while the three-year-olds delighted their grandma with the English version.

Why was this night different from all other nights? Passover celebrates freedom from the bondage we knew when we were strangers in a strange land.

There were my Chinese-Israeli cousins, my British son-in-law, my Californians, my Mossad agent swain. And the Seder plate crafted in Venice, stolen in Vienna, stored underneath an Italian monastery, spirited to Israel, and returned to my home in New York. Despite its splendor and the strife involved in retrieving it, what was on the Seder table was not nearly as important as who was gathered around it.

Uncle, released by my forgiveness before death from the burden of his terrible secret, joined us in spirit. And my mother, who let her daughter go. I wondered if they were finally together.

As the traditional "next year in Jerusalem" signaled the end of the ritual, my daughter announced that next year there would be one more of us. She was pregnant. As "mazel tov" rang out to her and Jonathan, I went over and hugged them with tears welling up. The life cycle—loss and gain. How thrilled Arthur and Uncle would be.

Marty, my editor at the *Smithsonian Magazine*, didn't think the story as it unfolded fit the assignment. He offered to extend the deadline and give me time to research the piece he wanted on the Judaica market. I took the "kill" fee and sold it to the *New Yorker*.

The article unleashed a flood of pent-up reaction among Holocaust survivors who had lost hope of ever retrieving art, bank accounts, life insurance benefits, and real estate illegally wrested from their families by the Nazis. Most could not afford the travel, legal fees, and time to pursue their property. Often, they didn't know where or how to start.

Uncle had left me a substantial portion of his estate, money I didn't need. I used it to establish a foundation to help finance the searches of others and a public registry of missing art to facilitate the process. It's based in Israel, with Ruth as the director.

Simon and I still keep company, as my mother's generation would say, though in her time our arrangement would be scandalous. We keep our own places. We joke that one problem about moving in together would be that his wardrobe is bigger than mine. But we spend most nights together, and we travel. I've also picked up a few nice new pieces of jewelry.

It's a comfortable and loving relationship. Marriage would be financially complicated, but Simon has called it a "foregone conclusion" that our future is together. My friends love seeing my picture in the *Times* Style section on Sundays.

But no one can go out every night. Sometimes we just stay home and eat gvetch.

Acknowledgements

WRITING A NOVEL perfectly illustrates Thomas Edison's concept of success: "90 percent perspiration and ten percent inspiration."

Inspiration for *After the Auction* originated more than 20 years ago from recollections of my late mother of a man she met during World War II. The character, Nachman Tanski, is a highly fictionalized adaptation of the small amount of factual information I was able to obtain about that long-deceased gentleman.

In the 1990s a flurry of books on Nazi art looting and headlines about families still trying to reclaim stolen property led to the founding of the International Art Registry, as well as new legal and museum standards and policies worldwide. This book was deliberately set before that resurgence of focus on this decades-old injustice. However, given the length of time *After the Auction* was a work in progress, I am indebted to the scholars who returned it to the world's attention.

Of these, Professor Jonathan Petropoulos of Claremont McKenna College has been a correspondent and friend, whose support has included clarification of the history, as well as validation of my book. I am deeply grateful. The work of Lynn Nicholas (*The Rape of Europa*) and Hector Feliciano (*The Lost Museum*) stand out as other research sources. D.P. Lyle, MD, answered my questions on the grizzly forensic aspects of the plot.

The "perspiration" element for this début novel came in the writing itself. Better late than never, I encountered Alan Rinzler, who taught me what a developmental editor is and does, and my gratitude to Alan for his guidance, judgment, and encouragement is boundless. K.D. Sullivan, another editorial professional and a friend, performed the unenviable task of "final" proofreading and introduced me to the talents of Dara England and Cecile Kaufman, whose work on cover design and book formatting, respectively, have enhanced the final product beyond my dreams or capabilities.

A group of friends and relatives read portions of early drafts, and over the years of this project people I know from the U.S. to China to Israel have rooted for it—and wondered if they were going to live to see it! These are treasured relationships for more reasons than the book and they continue to be the "jewels in the crown" of my life. Publishing a book makes me miss more than ever the enthusiasm and infectious giggle of my high school honors English pal and longtime friend, Beth Winnik Berkson, who died way too soon.

I wrote a hefty portion of one draft during a solitary stay at the Hidden Valley Writers' Retreat, my personal Yaddo in Santa Rosa, CA, thanks to my friends, Paula Simon and Howard Schoenfeld.

My parents, Sylvia and Robert Grossman, instilled in me the values of reading, history, and Judaism that inhabit this novel and created family travel memories that gave me a love for globetrotting adventure equal to theirs.

My son, Jonathan Ansfield, whose career as a foreign correspondent is the realization—a generation later—of an early ambition of mine, has always congratulated his mom "just for doing it"—whatever "it" was at the time—and such loving support from one's child represents the achievement of a much more valuable ambition.

My husband's son, Jon (my second Jonathan, as my son is his second Jonathan), treats me as his "mom" and cheers my activities. Right now he "can't wait to get the book" into his hands.

Supportive can be an overused word, but its model is my husband, Eli Frank. His love, generosity, assistance, and tolerance for all my activities—business, volunteer roles, the book—know no boundaries and make every day together a blessing.

Linda Frank
San Francisco, CA
March, 2010

Linda Frank is an author and businesswoman living in San Francisco. She has previously published business and travel articles in publications including *The Asian Wall Street Journal* and *The Forward* and produced and hosted a cable TV show. *After the Auction* is her first novel.

Breinigsville, PA USA
04 November 2010
248685BV00005B/2/P